The Last Window–Giraffe

A Picture Dictionary For The Over Fives

Foreword by Marina Abramović

Translation by Tim Wilkinson

SAN-
DORF
PAS-
SAGE

SOUTH PORTLAND | MAINE

Published by
Sandorf Passage
South Portland, Maine, United States

imprint of
Sandorf
Severinska 30, Zagreb, Croatia
sandorfpassage.org

Printed by
Stega Tisak, Zagreb

Sandorf Passage books are available to the
trade through Independent Publishers Group:
ipgbook.com / (800) 888-4741.

Library of Congress Control Number: 2023930589

ISBN: 978-9-53351-435-2

Foreword

By Marina Abramović

Peter Zilahy's award-winning novel uses the Hungarian alphabet to present a wonderful mix of historical facts, poetry, and visual images. His highly original approach was inspired by the time he spent in Belgrade in 1996, when citizens took to the streets to protest Slobodan Milošević's electoral fraud. As someone who comes from the former Yugoslavia, *The Last Window-Giraffe* evokes so many memories of my own past. There's a wizardry in Zilahy's ability to shrink an entire historical epoch to human scale while at the same time elevating ordinary experience to mythic significance. This is intellectual alchemy of the highest order, executed with wit and compassion. Zilahy can murder a sacred cow and canonize an unknown victim of totalitarianism in a single sentence.

"H" is for:

három puszi = three kisses
háború = war
harag = anger
halál = death
hatalom = power
hazudnak = they're lying

"U" is for:

úr = space
úr = blank
úr = nothingness

Péter Esterházy once wrote that Zilahy is the white raven of Hungarian literature who can observe the world each time as if for the first time, always fresh and original. While it's labeled a novel, the book is essentially uncategorizable, a hippogriff of a creation fashioned from fragments of history, autobiography, and wild invention. How such a wealth of elements—from childhood memories to political atrocities to the poignant evocation of the correspondence between sexual awakening and the deaths of dictators—could be gathered and spun into such a coherent narrative is a kind of aesthetic miracle.

The Last Window-Giraffe achieves this by brilliantly using humor. You cannot speak your mind under a dictatorship. So serious matters, matters of life and death, imprisonment and freedom, are addressed in jokes. And the biggest joke of all is that the dictators never understand this code of humor. But Zilahy does, so freely does he laugh and laugh at himself.

It is laughter at work, finding joy in the act of protesting, recognizing it as both political and performative, that makes this book read as timeless. There is much to learn here —yes, in terms of past, present, and future, but more importantly in terms of something far more essential that translates into any and all languages because it is at the heart of being human and something we all experience: living with the loss of innocence.

Love,

Marina

a

arany = gold
arc = face
akar = want
ablak = window
ablakzsiráf = window–giraffe
akasztófa = gallows
alkalom = chance

A is the first letter of the Hungarian alphabet.*

Through bulletproof glass darkly.

Disperse us though they may, I look him in the eye. Impassive muscle in shades, the vapour-trail of a glinting cigarette case. A golden age had been within arm's reach. We were ready to believe the Zastavas gliding by, our exiled fellow countrymen, that things were good there, like in a fairy tale, that it was not the West's lapdog, nor a nest of left-wing deviationists either, but non-aligned countries, Šurda, Dubrovnik, Opatija, the Sarajevo Winter Olympics. A window onto the sea, where the peace offensive did not block the vista. Where Albanians, Bosnians, Croats, Hungarians, Italians, Macedonians, Montenegrins, Romanians, Serbs and Slovenes all found land and water, pasture aplenty, hill and dale, as members of a federal republic. Their nostalgia fills me with envy, conjuring up the golden age of the Austro-Hungarian Monarchy. A is for *aurum*. Let this be the first window of my window–giraffe.**

I've long wanted to see the news live. To be familiar with the place and players, like watching a home movie of a school trip. In November 1996, the Yugoslav authorities tampered with the local election results. The frustrated populace of Belgrade took to the streets. In this dictionary you can learn many interesting things about Belgrade. You can also read out about the jungle on p. 13.

I first saw Seržan on CNN and later met him on the demonstration. He was conspicuous for his reticence. All that showed from under the cap that was pulled down over his ears were his teeth as he grinned. I could make out the Cyrillic letters on the book in his pocket and wanted to know why he was reading *One Hundred Years of Solitude* at a mass demonstration.

He wants to find the girl who lent it to him before the war. This is his chance to return it.

---

* A is the first letter of the Serbian alphabet. A is the first letter of the Croatian alphabet. A is the first letter of the Bosnian alphabet. A ≠ A.

** A popular primer in Hungary during the 1970s and '80s had the title of *Window–Giraffe: a Pictorial Encyclopedia* — those words representing the first and last letters of the Hungarian alphabet, A–Zs, with Ablak and Zsiráf being the first and last items.

Colonel Aureliano Buendía instigated thirty-two civil wars and was trounced thirty-two times. He survived fourteen assassination attempts, seventy-three ambushes, an execution, strychnine poisoning, and a suicide attempt. After the war he retreated to his alchemist's workshop and made goldfish from gold coins.*

In Belgrade, time is measured in faces. After a week, I began to recognize certain faces; in a year's time I would recognize everyone. Anyone who has a face also has the time. Watches are worn as ornaments, the hands enclosing an arbitrary angle that matches the wearer's mood. It's not possible for me to be late if I stay on the street. The time for the demonstration can be read off the faces. You look at someone and you know: it's time. Neither of you will get there on the agreed time, but you will meet somewhere else where you wouldn't have met if you had gone to where you were supposed to meet. Belgrade has escaped sidereal time. People look one another in the eye. They are whirling on a merry-go-round in a shower of confetti. A chain reaction of faces in a triggered explosion. Belgrade faces are incendiary, quick to flare up. It is impossible to become invisible. A Belgrade crowd is not faceless. Out of any two faces, one is always you. Seržan is an impudent grin. Belgraders cheerfully part with the past. A shared experience of disobedience and mischief, farting, belching, blowing whistles, honking horns. The old ducky standing next to me is yelling her head off. She knows it's allowed. Clocks have become historically redundant. Down with faceless time!

The *Window–Giraffe* was a picture book from which we learned to read when we didn't know

how. I already knew how by then, but I had to learn it anyway, because what else was school for. The *Window–Giraffe* made the world intelligible to us in alphabetical order. Everything had its rhyme and reason, symbolic or mundane. Thus, we could learn from it that the sun rises in the east, that our hearts are on the left, that the Great October Revolution took place in November, and that light floods in through a window–even when it is closed. The *Window–Giraffe* was full of seven-headed dragons, fairies, devils and princes, but it told us that these things do not exist. I remember four kinds of dragons that do not exist, and also three princes. The *Window–Giraffe* taught us to read between the lines. It was taken as much for granted as the teddy-bear on the children's bedtime TV programme. It didn't occur to anyone to question it. The window–giraffe was a window–giraffe. The *Window–Giraffe* is my childhood, the changing room, the PE class, the continual growing taller, the age before a better age, goulash communism, my homework, my innocence, my generation. The *Window– Giraffe* is a book one of whose characters was myself. It was only on being asked twenty years later that I realized the words of its title stood for the Hungarian alpha and omega. Yes, the *ablak —* window — is the beginning, the opening through which the light comes, whereas *zsiráf* — giraffe — is a bounded infinite — surrealism, flaming giraffes, we'll never die! A dictionary which contains what's been left out.

---

* 'Gold is a yellow-coloured metal. It is mined from the depths of mountains. Goldfish are not made of gold.'
  W–G, p. 7. *Ablak-Zsiráf — Képes Gyermeklexikon*, written and compiled by Ferenc Mérei. Budapest: Móra Kiadó, 1971. Original quotations from this text will be flagged by the abbreviation W–G.

There's a window–giraffe in Paris as well — I saw it on a postcard. It's called the Eye-fell Tower. It was sent by Sophie Brünner, who had defected to France with her parents and was now studying from a French reading primer. The Eye-fell Tower has a long neck, four legs, and an awful lot of windows: window and giraffe in one, even its name sounds good too, spur and promise in one, surpassing the *I'm-just-a-tot-I'll-grow-up-one-day* attitude of the nursery, a sudden leap, holding out the hope of a definitive break from the worm's eye view, which the express elevator down the middle reduces to a matter of technology. Sophie looked a bit like a giraffe herself, except she didn't have a window or an express lift down her middle. The express lift was in my throat when she tiptoed over to my desk on her matchstick legs and let me smell her fragrant eraser. That night I was in syllabifying ecstasies, with letters zooming into view like cat's eyes on a dark road. The next day, she defected. Our class teacher told us that her family had gone away unexpectedly. She might well have said 'was cut down in its prime', the way Party leaders go. The fragrant eraser left an indelible mark on my heart. Only later did we discover they hadn't gone off on a holiday at all, when as a proxy for herself she sent the Eye-fell Tower, which was just like a window–giraffe, except at least it made some sense to anyone who could read between the lines.

Aurum, ark, accident, art, alphabet, alchemist, archduke, Aurora, Arcadia, abracadabra

The cops are running in the opposite direction. We race past each other. They beat up a couple of passers-by on the other side of the square, then stand around in bewilderment. A pompous riot cop scrubs out a chalked gallows tree with his rubber stick. Below it, in red: Slobo, you'll swing for this, you pig!

'Péter wants to draw. He thinks of his coloured pencils and his sketch book. He stops playing, sits down at his desk, and starts to draw. He does what he wants.'* The crowd is protesting because it wants something else. Everybody wants something else. Free elections, freedom of the press, power, women, a Greater Serbia. No-one wants Milošević. They wish he did not exist.

á

ágyak = beds
ágyék = crotch
állam = state
állítólag = allegedly
álruhák = disguises

Beds run out in a city under siege. Katarina, an Italian journalist, sees the romanticism of '68 in the spectacle of her fellow correspondents dozing in the classrooms. So many sharing the same mattress! I wasn't alive then, so it is hard to pay attention to her. I had been woken up three times by Yugoslav border guards on the train, as if I had crossed three frontiers. I'm longing to get some shuteye, so I try to pass myself off as being someone important. By stressing my considerable experience with demos around the world, I'm given a bed in the old Jewish quarter.

---

* W–G, p. 5.

The dictator's private fortune is allegedly stashed in Cyprus. That is why the Mediterranean fleet has been put on alert.

The state decides when a state of emergency has supervened or exists. The state decides the state. A state can be tiny, pointed, oblong, , receding, protruding, double-chinned, flabby, fluffy, rosy or oval. A state can be a prison, a homeland, a haven. There are united states, friendly states, alliances of states. A state can suppress, civilize, grant privileges, integrate, sign mutual non-aggression pacts. A state can nationalize, imprison, single out for distinction, arm itself to the hilt, celebrate anniversaries of its existence. A state keeps tabs on its citizens: state examinations, state police, state security service. It decides what is not the case: false rumours, disguises, fallacies, victims. States fall. The state is statesmen, coups d'état, state finances. The state is a department store, restaurant, pub or café. The state is the state rail company, the Pioneers' Railway, the cog-wheel railway, the funicular to Buda Castle, the look-out tower on János Hill, Freedom Hill, the City Park, Margaret Island. The state is the Opera House, the Ballet Institute, the Sports Stadium, the Trotting Course, the Museum of Fine Arts, the Music Academy, the János Hospital, the Farkasrét Cemetery, the Érd Street Primary School. The state is a cinema, a barracks, a self-service restaurant, an archive, a cultural centre, a zoo, an amusement park, a circus, an ice rink, a children's camp, an orphanage, a retirement home, an institute for the blind. The state is the Centrum department store, the football pools and lottery, hardware shops, pawnbrokers, stationery, laundry, the Ervin Szabó Municipal Library. The state is an outdoor swimming lido. The state is a language. *L'état, c'est moi*, everyone who lives in it. The state is alone, it lives in constant fear, it makes friends, establishes diplomatic

Kabbala carved on double-leafed doors. After I left, apparently, Bibi Andersson slept in the same room and bed. Bibi Andersson played in *An Enemy of the People* and came to show her support for the students of Belgrade. On my next trip, lying on the let-down armchair of an unheated spare room, I thought of Bibi Andersson every night: *Passion, Persona* and *Hour of the Wolf.*

The poet compares the confluence of two rivers to a woman's crotch. Belgrade Castle is situated on the salient point at the confluence of the Danube and the Sava that old hands would consider the most sensitive spot on a woman's body. This is the point at which the fate of Hungary was decided five hundred years ago. Greater Hungary fell at Belgrade's clitoris. The defeat at Mohács five years later was just icing on the cake. A besieged castle that the Hungarians were once unable to defend, Belgrade is again a castle under siege today. For three months the attention of the news agencies has been directed towards this sensitive spot. A horde of voyeurs has tramped from the gentle slopes of the railway station to the precipitous wall of the Danube embankment to look down from there.

autumn, author, arse-hole, arsenal, Austro-Hungarian Empire, alarm, army, arm, alibi, ABBA, abacus, Addis Ababa contacts, reaches, rescinds and breaches international agreements, declares war, launches offensives, negotiates cease-fires and is a signatory over and over again. It is admitted to the community of nations. The state is a club, an exclusive society, state secret, state prosecutor, state interest, state religion. The state is scholarships, delegations, petitions, funerals, a craft. The state stands warranty, issues, collects taxes. The state is a financial institution: the state treasury, the state debt, government bonds, a government loan, state bankruptcy. A state can change its shape, size, language, religion, friends. The state is a border. The state is a state within the state. A state sometimes disintegrates into smaller states, in which case people try to put it together again.

b

babona = superstition
barátság = friendship
bűn = crime
BKV = Budapest Municipal Transport

A single ticket for the Balkan Express, student rate. She asks for my passport, I push it through the little slot in the window, beneath her glasses. You know you're no longer eligible for a student pass, she says. *Is that a question?* Couldn't you stamp it a bit further back all the same? I ask. Have a good look at me. I don't look a day over fifteen. She looks me up and down. I've got a nerve when my date of birth is right there. I'm not entitled to a one-third fare any more, and that's that. Do I really think I can trick the Hungarian State Railways? You surely don't take them for total idiots. Indeed, it never crossed my mind to think of the Hungarian State Railways as idiots, I swear. Budapest Municipal Transport — that's another matter. She casts a reproachful look: Hungarian State Railways, indeed! Filthy maybe, but not stupid. What would the world come to if everybody could get a ticket according to how old they looked, and she starts ticking me off as if I were fifteen.

I'm the only Hungarian on the train. The conductor warns me to lock the compartment door. Our boys (the cops!) will be getting off at the border. After that, God knows! I watch the stars through the spokes of the trees and, with my back to the engine, I softly hum *Every time Yugo* . . .

I vaguely recall from past reading that on leaving Budapest behind, both Leon Trotsky and Bram Stoker were thrilled at the approach of the Balkans. The war correspondent and the horror writer describe the countryside in much the same terms. Trotsky, travelling third class, believed he had discovered a Noah's Ark of nations. Both men's masterpieces sprang from this background: Dracula, and the Red Army.

I'm being bounced along, sleepless, a full-fare passenger on the Balkan Express. If I can't sleep, I have to drink, if I drink, I have to pee. The carriage is lurching, the train is slow on purpose. We've entered another time zone. A beer bottle is rolling outside in the corridor. I set off in search of the buffet in the direction the mouth points. From one of the couchettes come the sounds of a zither and a bagpipe. Hey-nonny-no! but I still ask where the buffet car is. They shake their heads in time to the music and roundly send me packing in every conceivable Serbo-Croat tongue.

In the summer we would sail on Lake Balaton. In winter the lake would freeze over, so we trained in Buda Castle. We did circuits of the ramparts,

running around the phallic gravestone of Abdurrahman, the last pasha of Buda, the turban on top of which I mistook for a globe. I made ambitious plans to circumnavigate the Earth without puking all over it. My sports injuries seemed to bear out the idea that the Earth is round and not flat. The nearest harbour was on the map. My great voyages of discovery began on p. 16 of the *World Atlas*. At first I mistook America for India, but my persistent wanderings over the map did not remain unrewarded. At the end of a game of Town, River, Mountain I noticed that capital cities beginning with B lie along a straight line between Brugge and Basra, from the North Sea to the Persian Gulf. The Brussels-Bonn-Bécs*-Budapest-Bucharest-Baghdad axis spoke for itself, and since I was aware that the birth of cities is also influenced by rivers, seas and mountains, I didn't think it fanciful to draw in Bratislava, Belgrade and Bern as well. Berlin's northern position may be regarded as a tectonic linguistic slippage, which the Great Powers corrected after the Second World War. My discovery seemed to be supported by other cities beginning with B that lie along the fault line: Breda on the Dutch-Belgian border, Basel and Bolzano in the Alps, Baden Baden in Baden-Württemberg, Bayreuth and Bamberg in Bavaria, Banská Bystrica in Slovakia or Brno in Moravia and Badacsony by Lake Balaton. Banja Luka in Bosnia may be stretching it a bit, but the line intersects Braşov in Transylvania. Having passed the Balkans, the linguo-tectonic fault line follows the Black Sea shore from Burgas in Bulgaria to the Bosporus, after which comes Istanbul, or Byzantium, and Bursa, the capital of ancient Turkey. Among the mass of Turkish towns beginning with B that are encountered on the way, it's worth mentioning Batman on the banks of the Tigris, as well as nearby Bitlis, for the anomalous currency of their names. Allowing for a short biblical bypass as we approach Beirut, we bag the cities of Byblos, Baalbek and Bethlehem, while the ruins of Babylon lie next to

* The Hungarian name for Vienna.

Baghdad. There was an obvious need to set out a morphological map that would prove the letter B had played at least as important a role in the growth of civilization as the big river valleys. From Babel to Brussels, history revolves around the axis of the letter B, from the unselfconscious burblings of a new-born babe to Banská Bystrica. A supranational globe took shape before my eyes, and I was confident that a suitable map and the application of speech therapy could lead back to that blissful pre-Babel era when all mankind spoke the same tongue. Given the frequency with which lines on maps have been altered over the last century alone, I felt I was on solid ground.*

Just before Belgrade a fog descends. If I didn't know we were in a valley, I'd take it for an ill omen. The fog is so heavy you can see no more than five or six inches ahead, and that's fog as well, with the rest of the fog behind it — and Belgrade too. Experience tells me the train will arrive and I shall get off.

Arriving in a strange city is a familiar feeling. Going as if you knew where you were going, as if you'd been there a hundred times before. Even cab drivers don't hail you. Paying attention to details, legs, clocks, street lamps, cigarette stubs, women's hats. Buying something, it doesn't matter what, you're not an outsider any more. Taking a seat on a bench and watching the movement, the colours, the proportions. Belgrade. I'm sure I have been here before.

'Fog is a cloud that is very close to the Earth. When we walk in fog, we are really walking in clouds.'**

---

*   See the map on p. 119. The fault line can be extended as far as the ocean via Birmingham and Belfast to the north-west, and via Bahrain and Bilad Bani Bu Hassan in Oman to the south.
** W–G, p. 83. For more on clouds: see the passage on p. 40.

During cocktails that evening I hear shooting. The next day, there are two wreaths at the crossing. From the newspaper, young lads in identical coats. I saw Janko Baljak's documentary about Belgrade's underworld: *The Crime that Changed Serbia*. By the time it was in the can, most of the actors had been killed. The cops let the hard cases leave the country during the Seventies. They were

given forged passports in exchange for a few trifling favours such as the liquidation of political opponents being made to look like accidents, and so on. As *Gastarbeiter* they would regularly go back home to spend their German marks, Swiss francs, and Swedish crowns in Yugoslavia. Then in the Nineties, war broke out with the new gangs. The reason there's no organized crime in Belgrade, a mafioso complains in the film, is because everyone is thinking short term. They'd rather shoot one another for peanuts than wait for a bigger deal. Yet it's just a matter of waiting. Take Bosnia, for example, and Arkan.

bad, badge, brother, butcher, Balkan, Belgrade, bomb, border, boredom, baksheesh, backlash, Bilbo Baggins

B is the third letter of the Hungarian alphabet. B is the letter of friendship. My first friend in Belgrade is Filip David. He is out demonstrating every day. He walks his dog in front of the police cordon. The dog is called Bilbo and is my second friend in Belgrade.

I didn't want to come to Yugoslavia during the war. A friend of mine was discharged from military service, where he was a top marksman.

His mother is half-Croat, half-Hungarian, his father is a Bosnian Serb. I didn't know which side he was fighting on, whether he had deserted or not, or even whether he was still alive. I didn't want to come within shooting range.

During the siege of Sarajevo, Saškija, a good boy, good soldier and the son of Radovan Karadžić, found himself face to face with a childhood pal called Jusuf. Jussie, an old-time gangster, had become one of the commanders of the resistance on Mount Igman. Yuka showed Saškija his wounds, and the good old days came up in conversation. Every night, Saškija would sneak across the Bosnian lines just to unwind a bit. They are reputed to have had a real bent for one another.

The riot cops are bussed in with packed lunches, like a bunch of out-of-town tourists. After a quick city tour, they form a cordon, march down Avenue of the Revolution and block off Republic Square. They have to wait hours before the demonstrators show up. In the meantime they buy roasted pumpkin seeds from street vendors, slip their rubber truncheon into the pinned-up groin flap of their body armour. Friendly passers-by tell them political jokes and hand out leaflets. Bimbos pin flowers on their shields and bring them cakes, which then become smeared all over their visors.

C

cetlik = paper slips
civil = civilian
ciki = naff

In films about the illegal Communist Party we saw earnest, gig-lamped but pretty girls accompanied by baby-faced working-class youths, strewing leaflets from factory chimneys, rooftops and train windows to worker-peasant-intellectuals who, after a furtive look around, would snatch them up and move on. Paper slips on the ground, in the air, stuck on to house walls. Endless torrents of reading matter with an educational or informative content — when and where we should go to protest, the planned schedule for the more interesting events and speeches, comic strips, sexually motivated solicitations. Celestial messages: 'Help the cops! Beat yourself up!'

civil, cynic, Cyrillic, cinema, cinnamon, CNN, circus, cigar, CIA, censor, cell, celestial

I buy dinars in the shoe shop. I'm being followed by plain-clothes cops. As if I were studying in Moscow in an old black-and-white film: drugstore in Cyrillic letters. A happy *Family Favourites* atmosphere reigns among the demonstrators. CNN tries to conduct a random vox pop of what the crowd would like for Christmas. The reporter asks a little old lady who has a cooking pot on her head. The answer is pithy but untranslatable, proclaims the interpreter after a moment's reflection. They're coming after me. They like my *ushanka* — that Russian hat with the tie-up ear flaps. Where did I get it? I'm from the West too, a bit embarrassing. My first clear Western thought is that I'm a bit naff. The UN is naff, NATO is naff and Yugoslavs know it. Not naff like the Warsaw Pact. There are rules that have to be observed. It works. There are civilized ways of doing things, after all. It comes from inside, an appearance of certainty. It feels right, even in the guts. Nonchalantly forgetting your wife's name, or building a mausoleum for your cat, wearing a white tie and tails when you go bomb-bomb-bombing along.

csonka = rump
család = family
csuromvizes = soaking-wet
csajok = chicks
csontok = bones

Rump Hungary and Serbia: 'You're Hungarian, you know how we feel.' Nostalgia as a *sine qua non*: Trianon and Dayton. Monument to a large and prosperous country. During the embargo, Budapest Ferihegy was the airport for Belgrade as well. The Hungarian ethnic minority in Yugoslavia never rose in revolt, the only ethnic group with any sense. All points in one's favour. It's good to be a Hungarian in Belgrade — a rare moment. Budapest and Belgrade have both been regularly razed to the ground. A shared historical experience. Defeated little nations with big mouths, melancholia, walled-off from the sea. Hungary even lost the very same stretch of seacoast. What's that if not a common lot?

'Péter set things straight. That is, he has made a mistake, but he put that right.'*

* W–G, p. 85.

9

The guests arrive soaking-wet and joke about whether drinking hot tea goes with water cannons. They know how to live. A burly historian got it full-force, the ice is melting from his beard. Mileta relates that  when he was young they stood with tiny flags beside Brankow Bridge and waved them at the dictators. He remembers Haile Selassie gliding by in an open car, the emperor of Abyssinia, who traced his ancestry back to King Solomon and the Queen of Sheba. Mileta holds a mirror up to the cordon: the fuzz watch themselves watching the demonstrators, who are watching the fuzz watching them.

Čeda, charm, chetnik, chance, cheat, chicks, chill, children, chant, chalk, challenge, Chain Bridge, checkmate

Čedomir reckons the opposition politicians have compromised themselves and have to be replaced. His favourite group is the Love Hunters. He doesn't trust journalists. And *L.A. Confidential* is the healthiest film to have come out of Hollywood. He draws my attention to Kim Basinger's monologue, adding that without Kosovo the Serbian people will have no living space.

A dishevelled girl student comes. She can't look him in the eye and bites her lip as she speaks. She has brought him a doll as a good-luck charm, to keep the cops away. Under her coat her knees are visibly quaking. Čeda nods, accepts the doll with a smile, but he still looks sad. Chicks bring him chocolates, cake and flowers, ask for his autograph and his hand in marriage. A protesting girl with a placard declaring Marry me Čeda!

Čeda is finishing drama school. He likes life in the raw, like Jean-Paul Belmondo in *Breathless* — that's the way to live. He goes around raising the students' spirits. There is a manifest abundance of girls and of high spirits. He drags his leg a bit, the artificial kneecap, a sports injury, hardly shows. He was a war correspondent in Slovenia. Čeda does not sleep, and that is more than ambition. He's a born leader, he doesn't take to bed when he has pneumonia. At dawn he addresses the shivering crowd, raising three fingers on high. They can't beat us, he says. A fly buzzes as he pauses for effect. With God's help we'll force our way through!

Čedomir is writing a play with the title *Death-Wish*. It's about the conflicts between father and son in the tempest of history. The father is the devil incarnate. Slobodan's very name is Freedom, capital F, and his eponymous Death-Wish (capital D) is the spur for an Oedipal storyline. The play also features a Beauty, capital B, who deserves to be made *ve-e-ry* happy, but circumstances are against her and she is obliged to sacrifice herself.

Slobodan Milošević's father was a secondary-school teacher of religious studies who was promoted to Russian teacher before he threw himself off a cliff in Montenegro. His mother hanged herself; his uncle, an army general, shot himself in the head with two guns, in stereo. One of the students' protest signs affirms the importance of keeping family traditions alive.

d

dobok = drums
diktátor = dictator
diákok = students
dugó = traffic jam

The standard slips out of Dugovics's sweaty palm. He tries to snatch it back. Suddenly he is gripped by doubt. Had he been a good father? A good husband? A good soldier? They grasp the standard at the same time. His chain mail gets snagged on the standard-bearer's talisman. Dugovics and the Turk atop the castle ramparts, seemingly immobile. Locked in a deadly embrace, each tries to trip the other. Two stag-beetles in amber. Dugovics is wrestling with time, with remembrance and forgetfulness. He sees a vast canvas in a museum, the picture being of him, in the same brown coat-of-mail. He resembles someone he had seen at the end of a pikestaff at the battle of Varna.

The official version has it that he had to drag the Turk with him in a death leap as the only way

of removing the Ottoman horse-tail standard from the castle wall. Many was the time on going to bed that I'd stare at the ceiling and imagine how I'd snatch the standard away from the Turk. I'd twist his arm behind his back, as they did to Nemecsek, the self-sacrificing hero of Molnár's *The Paul Street Boys*, or apply a full nelson as I did to Sohár when he chased me down the corridor with a pair of compasses. Maybe they had their hands full of banners, or maybe they dropped their swords at the same time, like in *Hamlet*. They could have been wrestling with hands bound behind them. Sohár, who had to repeat two years in school, surmised that Dugovics had probably leaned too hard against the railing while they were doing maintenance work. That's what had happened to one of his uncles, who fell into a lime pit. Contrary to vivid schoolboy folklore, Dugovics's name does not derive from the Hungarian verb *dug*, with its connotations of

'thrust', 'insert', 'conceal' and 'screw'. In Serbo-Croatian *dug* means 'tall', and this accords entirely with an article I read in a children's magazine which aimed to resolve the Dugovics issue once and for all. It claimed that tall and slim Dugovics was unable to push the stocky Janissary* off the rampart, and that's why he dragged him down with himself to their deaths. As a growing boy I was fascinated that someone's height might lead them to die a glorious death. Awesome. Dugovics's deed was symbolic and unrepeatable, like Hungarian history itself, his glorious death an eternal puzzle to every young schoolboy.

* Turkish foot soldier wearing uniform and receiving regular salary.

Across a distance of ten or twelve generations, he plunges to his death before our very eyes, an example of undiluted patriotism pure and simple. A nation plunges with him to its death, trying to yank Asia along with it: the Turks, the Tartars, the Golden Horde, the Soviets — fifteen million border guards of the Schengen Agreement, , fifteen million kamikazes left without an enemy. Defending Fortress Europe. The Hungarian suicide statistics.

drummer, Dada, Dayton, detective, dick, dictator, dictionary, dialogue, diarrhoea, diary, distance, disguise, dead duck, duty, Durex, drive-thru demo

On CNN Dušan — we last met a week ago — walks into Yugoslav army headquarters as a member of a student delegation. Cut. Then he makes a statement: the soldiers will not hurt the students. This time there will be no tanks on the streets. The talks proceeded in a friendly and

relaxed atmosphere, says CNN. The next time I saw Dušan in Belgrade I asked him what the army headquarters had been like. The generals were cracking jokes, he said, because one of the students had not yet done his military service, and they promised to send him to Novi Pazar, which is like Grimsby, except it's grimmer. When

he was enlisted, incidentally, Dušan drove a tank, but he kept quiet about that in front of the generals. He talks about responsibility, he's afraid someone might get hit, he can't sleep properly. A madman might show up any moment, and if anything happens, they'll blame him. After all, Gavrilo Princip was a Belgrade student.

A party in the diplomatic quarter. Over grappa and smoked salmon, we argue about why the students are protesting. Because they are students?

'The drummer beats a drum. He beats it with a drumstick.'*

My bumpy road to sexual maturity was paved with the deaths of Communist dictators. My first sexual experience coincided with the death of Mao Zedong: I was bitten by a girl called Diana in nursery school. My voice broke when Tito died, and I had my first ejaculation when Brezhnev went. For three days all they played on the radio was classical music, which I thought was rather overdoing it; some schools were even closed. Then for a long time there was nothing. As an experiment, I took a girl to the movies, but the film was too good, and I got a cramp in my hand. Events accelerated at high school. There were only a couple of months between the first kiss and the first frantic fumblings. After Andropov Chernenko quickly checked out. A few more weeks and it was Enver Hoxha's turn, but I'd rather not go into that. I first found out about the G-spot when Ceaușescu was executed. Kim Il Sung cast new light on my broadening horizons. Luckily, the charges were dropped. Now as for Fidel . . .

Everyone sets off home simultaneously at a deliberate slow march, with government supporters tooting their horns. We shuffle slowly forwards. There's gridlock, a motorized demonstration. In Belgrade, one can even take the car on a demonstration. Utterly American! A drive-thru demo!

---

* W–G, p. 152.

12

The happiest traffic jam I have ever seen. Half the city are killing themselves with laughter. We are putting the brakes on time. Even the pedestrians are beginning to slow their pace on the pavement. A pantomime protest. People lean into a curve and fall on top of one another. They can't stand it any more, you can't laugh slowly.

Milovan Đilas, Tito's friend, did nine years in two halves. During the half-time interval, he had a year and a half on parole. Over the nine years he was allowed one hundred and sixteen visits of half an hour each: his wife kept tabs on it. His son lives across the street. I go over to see him. Alex is busy as he works for a TV foreign affairs programme, but he's got half an hour for me. The conversation gets off to a good start. Alex calls the Hungarians the greatest losers of all time. At least I don't have to make any excuses. A brief digression by way of Hungary's suicide rate, Mohács, Kosovo, Trianon, and we're soon fast friends. His father persuaded Tito to allow jazz. Stalin liked

him and wanted him to replace the Marshal, but Đilas happened to mention that Red Army soldiers had raped the womenfolk of Belgrade during their siege of the city at the end of the Second World War. He couldn't keep his mouth shut. He was arrested in 1956 because he objected to the Soviet occupation of Hungary. When they searched his apartment they found his gun, a gift from Marshal Konev. A bullet rolled away. Alex had picked it up and tried to pack it into his toy gun. They were taking his father away. Đilas's last image of his home: the goons laughing at his son's attempts to load his popgun.

dz

'Dz is the seventh letter of the Hungarian alphabet. There is no Hungarian word beginning with dz.'*

'Dzo (or zho or zo)', a Tibetan loan word, is the genetic and linguistic product of crossing a yak with common cattle. 'Pure' yaks can only be seen in a zoo. The dzo is a domestic animal, which means that every single dzo is a hybrid, and they are becoming more hybrid as time goes by. A civilized herd, every member of which looks different. Chinese scientists are now trying to extract what little yak remains in the dzo.

Sarajevo Zoo was a no-man's land during the siege. Caught in the crossfire, the keepers were afraid to feed the animals, whose ethnicity was uncertain to begin with. Having been forced into a ghetto, the animals were unable to come up with a suitable response to the challenge of civilization. The giraffes were the first victims, since they couldn't duck fast enough.

dzs

dzsungel = jungle

Zoran Đinđić, the democrat. There was an article about him in *The Washington Post*. The leader of

* W–G, p. 33.

the best organized opposition party, a future president of Yugoslavia, a hunk. Đinđić did time under the old régime, then he was granted a German scholarship. At the start of the war he supported Vuk Drašković. His party platform includes a Greater Serbia and also raises the subject of family planning for Albanians. A multimillionaire friend admits to going to see him in Germany long ago. Zoran already knew how to live back then, he says, he was always surrounded by great women. Đinđić is demonstrating with his son on his shoulders. Along comes Vuk and kisses the child. One big family.

For jungle: see rainforest (p. 73).

e

ellenség = enemy
ellenzék = opposition
erőszak = violence
egyensúly = balance
el nem kötelezett országok = non-aligned countries

Mileta Prodanović recounts an episode from the history of ethnic wanderings in the Balkans. In the sixteenth century, the Klementi, a tribe of Catholic Albanians, fled northwards to the Muslim Sanjak of Novi Pazar. They converted to the true faith and adopted the language of the surrounding Serb populace. One group wandered further north to the province of Srem, where they reconverted to Christianity and accommodated the language and customs of the local Croats. With an influx of Serb refugees from Croatia in 1993, however, the ethnic scales tipped in favour of the Serbs. During an impromptu celebration, the new mayor of the small town of Hrtkovci renamed the streets. On unveiling the new signs, he condemned the past. The street named after Ustasha leader Vladimir Nazor* was given the name of Tsar Stephen Dušan, while the one named after Ustasha agent Bishop Josip Juraj Strossmayer** was restyled Prince Miloš Road. And finally Sándor Petőfi, he said, then paused . . . the path of whose life is alien to us, let his street be known from this day on as King Péter Avenue. Little did he know that Hungary's star nineteenth-century poet was the son of a well-known Chetnik butcher called Petrović.

Sundown with police cordon, the light dancing on the shields. A guy comes along who's hurrying to his sick mother and asks the cops to let him through. She lives just over there, in that house, otherwise he'll have to make a big detour. He's waved away. A dog comes up and snarls. The cordon opens up.

We didn't notice, but it has been here all the time. They've been standing here all along, and only now do we notice how many of them

---

* Communist poet and partisan hero in World War II.
** A liberally inclined Catholic bishop who defied the papal authority in siding with Orthodox Christians.

there are, all at once, in one spot. Now at least we can see them face to face. It took this many of us to face the cordon, this many people wanting at the same time to know for sure that this is not what we want. They aren't going to hurt us, they just won't let us pass. We can stay here or go home, it's just that we can't go the one way we want. Everyone individually can move around without let or hindrance, but together we are helpless. Wherever we head, a cordon forms as if we were prisoners of an invisible field of force, captives of the country, even though I can leave any time I wish.

Three together, two men and a woman — all three beaten up, which is why they're still together. A populist, a pragmatist, and a Europhile. Together: Zajedno — the name of the opposition.

French politician Jack Lang's visit to Belgrade caused a stir in the media. Lang came to show his solidarity with the student demonstrators. The Belgrade opposition had two good reasons to invite him. For one thing, having been a student leader in '68, he'd be sure to see eye to eye with the students. For another, having been France's minister of culture, he might be able to help secure funding for their cultural institutions. Lang's pilot, who didn't have an entry visa, was detained at the airport and spent the rest of his time drinking coffee with four agents, who kept him under close surveillance. What could the pilot have possibly found out when, apart from these four men, he had only gained a bird's-eye-view of Belgrade as hundreds of thousands were marching on its streets demanding free elections?

Lang is easy-going and accommodating by nature, a leftist, but the kind of man even Giscard could get along with. He makes statements, delivers speeches, delights his hosts. When he arrives at the students' headquarters at the university a group of history and philosophy majors ask him to follow them upstairs. On the fourth floor he is told that he will not be going to give a speech of any kind, because he signed a UN motion that demanded the bombing of Belgrade during the war. Lang doesn't throw a fit. Instead, he tells them he's never heard of any such document, then asks if Kafka was, by any chance, a Serb. The philosophy students, failing to appreciate his Gallic wit, surround him and insist that he leaves the building instantly. CNN and Reuters failed to secure interviews from the rapidly retreating Lang, who at least saved a pilot from caffeine poisoning that day.

In a lift the next day, I met an eye-witness and asked him what he thought about the Lang affair. What did I mean? Lang hates the Serbs, didn't I know that? Lang is an enemy! Coming from a friendly country myself, I know all about ideological warfare. Lang was a Maoist in '68. A student leader turned minister of culture. Know your enemy to learn who you are!

ego, echo, ethno, enemy, evil, evolution, EU, euphoria, euphemism, eleven, ember, embarrass, embryo, episode, error, encyclopedia

A non-aligned tale. Maria lived on the right bank of the river, in Austria, Franjo on the left bank, in Hungary. Franjo would cross the river to steal firewood, and since the two countries were one nobody was bothered when Maria and Franjo fell in love. They were as poor as church mice, they starved, they were cold, eight of their children died. But that still left seven, and Maria hoped that her seventh son would become a priest. Franjo wanted to send him to America, but he couldn't raise the four hundred crowns needed for the passage. Josip was conscripted into the Imperial and Royal (Kakanian) Army. He fought, was taken prisoner, and escaped. In the summer of 1917, he tried to leave Russia via St. Petersburg, so that from Finland he could take a ship bound for America. He was caught and served time. America sailed away. Revolution broke out, the Great October one, then came the Soviet Union and a fresh opportunity. He married a Russian woman and met a worker from the Putilov factory, who recruited him into the underground movement. He was wearing spectacles as a disguise when he returned to his native village, and through these glasses he saw that the river no longer divided Austria and Hungary, but Slovenia and Croatia, yet this bothered nobody because the two countries were one. He rose through the ranks of the movement's hierarchy, passed through a succession of jails, became a hunger striker, a guerrilla leader, and then president of Yugoslavia. When Stalin sent assassins after him, he lost all interest. The Soviet Union sailed away, too. He now longed for a Third World, something that would be both East and West without being either. He looked at the map and discovered the non-aligned countries. He toured the globe as the uncrowned king of the Third World, and there was even a film made of his life with Richard Burton playing him. In a television interview before he died, he said not everything had happened quite the way it had been recorded. His diamond ring twinkling on the screen, the dictator, now eighty-odd years old, gives the impression of being a satisfied man. Tito didn't live to see Yugoslavia win gold in basketball at the 1980 Olympics, nor the end of the Second World — let alone a time when the little river which had once divided and brought his parents together would become a real border.

'When we let something go, it never stops.'*

é

élni = to live
éjszaka = night
éjjelilepkék = death's-head moths
és én? = what about me?

The enormous park at my nursery school was full of secret hiding places. Most of the things are probably still where I hid them. I found a death's-head moth behind the hedge and hid it among the dead leaves. I thought it was a toy, but it flew off at dusk. Life took it away from me. Never mind, though, I was getting ready for a big deal, teaching my kitten how to fly. I stood at the head of the cellar stairs and explained to him what he had to do, then — wheee! Living

"And Now for Something Completely Different!"
Belgrade 1996-97

* W–G, p. 126.

things are unpredictable. My death's-head moth collection was growing: cats, dogs, turtles, friends, relatives, lovers are flying around above the city. I'll come back for them.

Organic buildings, with human lianas at the windows, whistling, gesturing, flashing pocket lamps like so many animated caryatids and putti. Sales assistants are standing in shop windows, staring out, the shop-window dummies are waving. Construction workers cheer and brandish hammers on the scaffolding. A man leaning out from a fifth-floor balcony swings a three-branched candelabra in the air as if he were about to cast an anchor into the crowd swimming below him. The streets turn into river valleys. I let myself be swept along. A woman flings her arms around my neck, but I don't speak Serbian. No matter, she loves me just the same.

'O life! How sweet it is to be alive!'*

The doctors decided my due date was November 7th, the anniversary of the Great October Revolution. My mother declared that she was going to hold out for one more day even if it killed her.**

ex, exile, extreme, exhume, exaggerate, experiment, excrement, excuse-me, example, exotic, exit

bottle of slivovitz into my hand. The soundtrack from Emir Kusturica's film *Underground* is booming from a couple of speakers. If you want to stay alive, you dance. The riot cops are replaced every hour. They get extra for a night shift, like snow-clearance workers. They don't drink, don't dance, are just rooted to the spot in the subzero temperature, fuelled by hate. The demo is run like a picnic. You have to eat if you want to break through. Sandwiches, chocolate wafers, lemon curd tarts, four kinds of drinks. Two students come along to say there's going to be tear gas. Does anyone have a gas mask, or do we know where to lay our hands on any: it won't be a picnic without one. They go off in search of some. And I thought I was ready for anything! The wind picks up, so it seems there won't be tear gas after all, and anyway the cops are preparing to leave. Whistles, applause, cheers. The city opens up at one a.m. Five hundred set off, and an hour later there are thirty thousand of us. Cigarette lighters and candles in the windows, room lights being switched on and off. We march through the city to the sound of drums. We pelt the Milošević residence with snowballs. The snow soon runs out, but we've still got plenty of balls. Three plain-clothes men drive into the crowd, but they get out in one piece. A disciplined demonstration. Going on till three a.m., beer with vodka chasers is the rule: general euphoria, we progress in dance step. We go to places where no demonstrators have ever gone

A bottle is passed around, no glasses, but there's a promise of whisky if we are good. We're bracing ourselves against the cold. It's minus five Celsius outside. I'm not dressed properly for a demonstration, I just popped out to take a look at that night's cordon. Someone presses a

---

* W–G, p. 42.
** 'Check the calendar to see on which day your birthday falls this year, and on which day May the First falls!'
  W–G, p. 104.

18

before, narrow streets, residential areas, then swing back into the centre via Avenue of the Partisan Brigades. Right then a thirty-foot banner being carried at the head of the procession doesn't seem overstated: BELGRADE IS THE WORLD! Someone passes me a fag. I join the human ribbon, stepping in time to a poem by Christian Morgenstern: 'A knee treks lonely round the globe. / It is a knee, that's all! / It is no tree! It is no wardrobe! / It is a knee, that's all!'

f

fürdetés = bath time
foci = footie
forradalom = revolution
feketefehér = black-and-white
fej vagy írás = heads or tails

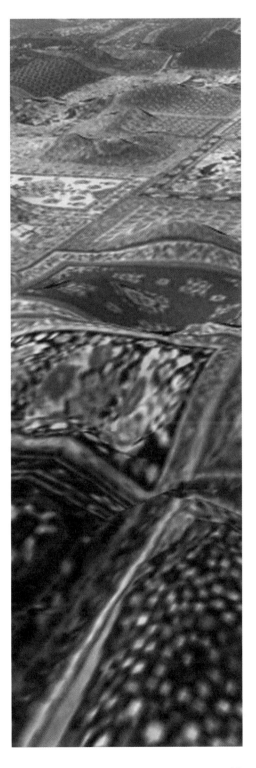

My bath time was during the early evening news. Mum would look in, every now and then, to check that I was all right, while Dad watched the TV in the living room. In order to be able to protect me from the lies they had to be aware of the details. In the bathroom all that could be heard were Mum's sighs — what a mess I was making, flooding the apartment. I would submerge myself, and under the water a voice would speak to me, telling me what had happened in the world that day: a landslide had buried a hundred and fifty people in Bangladesh, revolution had broken out somewhere in West Africa, a new nursery school and an Olympic swimming pool had been opened, and MTK had beaten Ferencváros 2:1. I had no idea who was sending the messages, or why, but clearly they had plans for me because they also told me what the weather would be. The next day I was able to distinguish several voices in the tub, which suggested I was dealing with an organization. This manner of communication seemed logical. I couldn't send them messages, because you can't talk under water, and they could only get in touch with me without my parents and teachers knowing during my bath time. I found it hard to grasp why it was so important for the organization that I should have a detailed low-down on the latest war games in Poland, or which Transdanubian communities were being granted municipal status, but I knew that if I paid attention, sooner or later they would give a sign. My life gained a deeper meaning under water. One Sunday, when Mum was washing my hair and, unwittingly, dipped my head into the water, a pleasant female voice whispered in my ear that the harvest had been flattened by hail. I knew what was expected of me, and to be honest, I had no objections: to make a big mess. Even before then, I had been in the habit of battling with submarines and fighter planes in the dark, after going to bed, and sometimes I would end up on the floor, so it was only thanks to my doggedness that victory was mine in the end. From that day on, I was busy as a bee sabotaging the development of our people's democracy. Earthquakes, power failures and gas explosions marked my path. I would figure out military objectives on the basis of intelligence I received in the bathtub. When a factory or a power plant was inaugurated, I would be there, doing what I had to do. Comecon fiddled at repairs behind the Iron Curtain, little suspecting that a stone was being thrown inside the glass house.

I was a virgin, but that didn't bother me. I didn't have a clue. The world was black-and-white, you could see it on TV. I can still see, as if before my eyes, the extra time played by Argentina and Holland in the '78 World Cup, the Baader-Meinhof and Salyut-Apollo link-up, the death of the King (I didn't know who Elvis was, but Dad was choked), the ash cloud over Mount St. Helens, 'Bertie', Farkas the first Hungarian in space, and the World Rubik's Cube Championship in Budapest. Sports were exciting in black-and-white. In a boxing match you had to tell the boxers apart by counting the stripes on their socks. I even remember how many stripes my first date had. I'm not sure about the colour of the eyes, even now I see her in black-and-white. After the first kiss my parents bought a colour TV, and it turned out that the Dutch are orange, whereas the Italians are blue, and there are even red devils. Only the Germans remained black-and-white, as if they were being punished. Their country was split in two as well. I almost felt sorry for them.

Milošević's son is a racing driver, he crashes Ferraris. Flying a Ferrari flag for fun is on a par with marching with employees from the May 1st Clothing Factory on a May Day parade. A symbolic opposition camp in Belgrade demonstrates with Brazilian flags bearing Ayrton Senna's picture. How many more Ferraris does he have to crash before he catches up with Senna?

We stop for a beer between two demonstrations. The fuzz are warming up in leisurely fashion on Terazije, checking their Doc Martens, forming into a line. The protesters are slowly gathering. Someone produces a ball and they start kicking it about in front of the police cordon. The hard core arrives. Red Star Belgrade fans with flags, car horns, drums. "Ere-we-go, 'ere-we-go, we're coming through!' they shout at the three thousand cops.

The TV sports reporter within you stirs, and you start giving a running commentary to those standing next to you. Viewers, today we shall find out what advantage playing at home gives. Milošević's squad has been beefed up, but it might just be in for a surprise from the side streets. Don't assume the visitors are unbeatable. There are rumours of transfers and bad blood in training camp. The home team gains possession from the throw-in, but the cops try to block play with rapid interceptions.

There's a melee in the centre, the clearance is late, the defenders are pulling the opposition towards themselves, a gap appears in the wall, Puskás shoots and . . . It's a goooo-oal!

The revolution must be kept going, Tito said. Bulevar Revolucije — Avenue of the Revolution — is the longest thoroughfare in Belgrade, for all that there has not yet been a revolution in Belgrade. The protesters throw rotten eggs at the Television Centre, the offices of government newspapers, and the Radio building. The eggs are pierced with a needle and then left to stand for three days. When the stench becomes unbearable, it's time to throw them. Egg grenade à la Belgrade — it's all in the timing. Wider tactical application of this weapon is deterred solely by the sky-high price of eggs. Nevertheless, its memory is preserved by folklore, with its name sticking to the demonstrations like rotten eggs to the wall: the Yellow Revolution.

On the eve of Hunyadi's raising of the Turkish siege of Belgrade, the defenders lit fires to the greater glory of Christianity on the Danube bank at Zemun. From the further bank, the thousands of bonfires look like an unbroken sea of flame. Every time the Turkish pipers starts up, the Crusaders set up an ear-splitting din with trumpets, drums, horns, zithers, bells, pots and pans and shields. They couldn't tolerate unison.

The tough nuts march under a Brazilian flag, chanting football slogans. Behind them comes a column bearing the images of saints and leading politicians. Little more than a few steps separate Saint Sava and Vuk Drašković. The activist who was brought back from death makes a speech; he is still willing to die for the cause. Too late. Two effigies in this fancy-dress procession win popular approval: one is a red monkey, the other Milošević in convict's garb. Three generations dance hand in hand in front of the police cordon, like excited debutantes. The immediate risk of punishment makes their movements crudely

erotic. Jiving teenies flinging themselves around to rock and roll, pensioners waltzing in tender embraces. Female students tease the riot squad: Are you dancin'? A young cop quips: Sorry, they're not dressed for the occasion. It's getting dark. They carry on by the glow of cigarette lighters. The flames are mirrored on the policemen's visors. Lights in surrounding apartments are flicked on and off. The star atop the tower block of the City Hall shines out ruddily, glistening sheets of ice on the Danube. Belgrade, city of light.

fun, fuzz, flood, fear, fever, fame, family, Ferrari, flags, flash-lights, fire-lighters, faces, facts, fanatics, fetish, fair play, Franz Ferdinand

In Bosnia they found a bunch of photos of decapitated heads carried by Saudi POWs. It was only the pictures that they collected, not the heads. Heads sundered from the body, flying and rolling heads, peaceful and angry countenances. On being questioned, they said they intended the shots to serve as evidence, they were no murderers. Everyone needs a hobby. Head-hunting or photography? Identifying with your subject, capturing the moment between life and death, checking the focus. Watch the birdie!

g

gumi = rubber
gén = gene
gödör = pit
golyó = bullet

'Rubber trees grow in the jungles of far-off hot climates. When their bark is slit, raw rubber oozes out. The raw rubber is turned into car tyres, gumboots, rubber balls and rubber erasers in the rubber factory.'* You can read more about the jungle on p. 73. The rubber sticks — *gumibotok* — that the cops carry are also made from raw rubber. In fact, riot cops carry loads of other equipment that begins with the letter G: *géppisztoly* (machine gun), *golyóálló mellény* (body armour), *gázálarc* (gas mask), *könnygáz-gránátvető* (tear-shell launcher).

Through bulletproof glass darkly. To look at the past. A golden age slipping by, the backs of the cops, the driver's face in the mirror. To memorize a Swiss bank account number. To go around in sunglasses in

* W–G, p. 58.

Romania had just won its twentieth gold. If it hadn't been for Trianon*, there wouldn't have been a single Hungarian medal in Los Angeles. I was sent off court to the end, fuming with belated revolutionary fervour. It was as if the referee's coded objectivity — personal foul — was confronting me with the failure of my very existence. In the locker room I sought death in vain, my shoe strings were too short. It's all in the genes, Dražen explained after the game, which was when I first saw a Pioneer slam-dunk the ball. Yugoslavs are all geniuses, he went on, they invented everything: the ballpoint pen, for example, the safety match, the airship. He reeled off a bunch of familiar-sounding names, and facts go well with someone who can grasp a basketball in the palm of one hand. The linking of sport to science piqued my curiosity; for a while I supposed they taught genetics at the Institute for Sports.

winter. To own the media. To know how to win elections.

There's a television built into the back seat. He watches how he is being shown, sitting inside, from the outside in live transmission. He switches channels, but he's on all stations.

games, gums, guns, guards, grenades, gallows, gas masks, graffiti, goal, galore, Guevara, Golem, guillotine, Golden Team, Guantanamera

The Yugoslavs were a head taller, had a spaceship on their vests, and wore size forty-six trainers. The shadows were lengthening on the playing fields at Csillebérc children's camp on the outskirts of Buda. Dražen leaned leisurely on my aura. I didn't want to punch him in the solar plexus . . . no, I went for the throat. That's when they introduced the three-point rule. It hadn't been long since my voice had begun to break. It all happened so suddenly. I asked for a time out: an eternity under the backboard. I'm still growing, and they're casting a shadow on my glory; in my hand is a scrap of a Yugoslav singlet. The 1984 Olympics were on telly at the time — the Games our Party and government boycotted.

I dreamt of the day when I, too, would grip the ball between finger and thumb, my little finger crooked. I knew the Golden Team off by heart: Divac, Paspalj, Raða, Kukoč, Petrović, Vranković, Danilović, Grosics, Puskás, Czibor . . . ** Gods in their own right. A Third World All-Star team, non-aligned basketball. They gouged, elbowed, pinched, bit, cooed sweet nothings in their opponent's ears, cursed fluently in every tongue from the Baltic states to Aramaic. Unforgettable trips and immaculate shoves. A morality of a higher order was manifested in their surprise attacks, partisan nerve in the face of superior forces: the will — and the daring — to win even if it meant breaking the rules.

* In 1920, under the Treaty of Trianon, Hungary was reduced to a third of its size and lost five million native Hungarians.
** Stars of Yugoslavia's basketball squad in the late Eighties — except for the last three, who were footballers in Hungary's own Golden Team (among other things, they beat England 6:3 at Wembley in 1953).

I looked up to Yugoslav basketball. It gave me strength when times were hard. When I was weighed and measured, for example, under the pretext of a physical. I had to stand under a pole that was disproportionately taller than me, was made to take my shoes off and had a bar lowered onto my head. By the laws of physics, it ought to have come to rest at my skull, but this chopper sloped backwards, cutting inches off my height. My hair was also cropped short then so I would have no defence. No use my standing on tiptoe, I would be thrust back on my heels. Then just when I was beginning to think my head had stuck somewhere between my legs, they would whisper into my ear an arbitrary number around waist height — just to test me.

I knew there was a conspiracy against time, and it was up to me to warn the world that genetic experiments were being carried out here on young Pioneers, the Helsinki Accords being violated, pygmies trained for mine sweeping. I drew a swastika on the school wall, and I was the one charged with finding the culprit. That's when I realized that all my life I would be expected to dish the dirt on myself and hand my own head over on a silver platter. The system was inhuman, and in exchange for my silence the best I could do was be my own scapegoat. First I needed to give myself up, then I could grow up — no thank you! I wanted the whole world. All they're after is to wake the sleeping lion, and make me blow high school and higher ed. I'm not gonna be their fall guy. I know what I want. I'm gonna be a genetic engineer, I'm gonna strike back.

'At school, Péter answers his teacher's questions with pride. He speaks out clearly and stands up straight.'*

I saw them installing the blue neon lights. I didn't know what the sign meant, but there was something fundamentally positive about the centenary neon gleam: 'One Hundred Years

of MOM.' So, the prospects were good, this was a place in which to live and die. And it went on like this for years. The Hungarian Optical Works stayed one hundred years old and didn't age. You could see the sign from all parts of town, even at night: still one hundred years old! We vied over who could read it from farthest away. It was one of the Budapest fixtures: the stone lions of the Chain Bridge, the Marx-Engels-Lenin triptych, and the one-hundred-year-old MOM. This year, though, I thought my eyesight had begun to fail. There was a big pit where the factory had stood, and people at the fence around the site just goggled. Whatever had happened to the one-hundred-year-old

MOM? The works had been blown up along with the neon sign, and in its place was a pit so huge you could see it from outer space, like the Great Wall of China. 'Bertie' Farkas, Hungary's one and only astronaut, stares round-eyed: One Hundred Years of . . . BOOM! MOM had just gone with the wind. Surely you didn't think it was going to last for ever?

The news came in concurrently, in late June 1991, that Yugoslavia had won the European basketball championship and invaded Slovenia.

* W–G, p. 17.

The Slovene player was missing from the team in the final. By then the tanks were on their way down the Fraternity and Unity highway. The old wound had suddenly opened up, and we watched helplessly from under the backboard as the southern Slav Golem shattered into a multiplicity of small nations. The mythical partisan army had vanished into the mist, the Yugoslav brainchild was dead, its cheekiness and ingenuity melted away into the world order. I no longer knew who to cheer for.

Since then I have grown up, and now I know it is Hungarians who are the geniuses. It was Hungarians who invented the airship, the ballpoint and the safety match — they're just everywhere! Here's an interesting fact about the siege of Byzantium. In accordance with his plans for racial integration, the sultan used European gunners as mercenaries. Back then — let's not be bashful, the best cannons were cast by a Hungarian, the Áron Gábor, or János Irinyi or Ede Teller of his day. He had offered his services to the Greek emperor, but they couldn't agree to terms. Geniuses are not easy to get on with. Master Orbán's cannon was pulled by sixty oxen and fired stone cannonballs weighing almost half a ton. A charge of over four hundred pounds of gunpowder was needed for every single round. How that shot smashed all previous records, a quantum leap like when Mike Powell broke Beamon's record in Mexico City — the oldest

mark in track and field athletics. Constantinople — one thousand years old — was blown to smithereens, dissolved into thin air like the one-hundred-year-old MOM. The wall between East and West fell in 1453, five hundred years before Berlin. I can't stress the Hungarian contribution enough: a Gyula Horn, a King Stephen, a Béla IV. Byzantium is plundered, and before you know it we have *Gastarbeiter*, shish kebab, Turkish baths, the tomb of Gül Baba, coffee, tobacco, whips, and stuffed cabbage. Orbán smashed the gates open, and the Spirit of the East marched into Europe: a Csoma de Kőrös, an Arminius Vámbéry, a Franz Liszt.

One sporting history puzzler is worth a thought. What would have happened at Marathon if a Scythian inventor had turned up on the Persian side? How many kilometres would runners have to cover today?*

gy

gyakran = often
gyerekek = children
gyakorlati órák = craft classes

On 24 December, they're handing out pedestrian licenses to the demonstrators. The city's full of people running amok. Counter-demonstrators have a different way of walking. They circle alarmingly, constantly come the other way and carry posters of Milošević, which is just asking for trouble. They stroll into pedestrian streets against the flow. Sunday drivers. After the fuzz intervened, fear coupons made an appearance, on the model of postwar food coupons.

---

* The Scythians, who nomadised the southern Russian steppes, were once popularly thought to be the ancestors of the Magyars.

I managed to lay hands on four coupons, and I practically shat a brick when I saw the police in gas masks. The cops are slowly running towards us. Is this in the rules, I wonder?

My first childhood memory is of crawling on all fours during the rest period at nursery school. The curtains are drawn, and there's a moon shining on the white blankets. It can't be the Moon itself, of course; we were never there at night. Anyway, I'm crawling on all fours under the beds, afraid that if the others wake up, then I shall wake up as well. I am alone, a near-fictitious child, balancing on the creaking parquet floor, breadcrumbs drilling into my kneecaps. I'm small and nobody notices me. I'm worming my way along the enormous room as if I had been doing it for hours. I'm dodging hands and feet that are dangling out from under the white sheets. Dead tired little angels. Formations of fleecy clouds float past, podgy fingers, dimples, curly locks. Uh-oh! Somebody's coming the other way under the bed. Our heads bump, but because of the sheet I don't see the face. She's panting on my neck, hot breath. The nursery assistants are coming in their white overalls, white socks and white slippers. We crouch under the bed, her little hand grasping my little hand. Her palm is sweaty.

The demonstration in Belgrade is a family affair. If you're not careful, you might knock a child over. There are children on shoulders, in laps, walking hand in hand, mothers protest with Pampers tucked under their arms. Baby-faced students and riot cops. Since the demonstration began everyone's been worried about the children. The children of Party members are also demonstrating. According to polls, three-quarters of the parents were '68-ers. In 1968 the students of Belgrade demonstrated for a tougher Communism, carrying posters of Che Guevara. There are claims on TV that the students are being manipulated, so one new badge that has become all the rage proclaims 'I'm a manipulated student.' A more radical version runs: 'I'm an immature, underage, manipulated, fascist student, and I feel great.' Terry Gilliam, one-sixth of 'Monty Python's Flying Circus', has sent the students a letter of encouragement: 'Hold out! The whole world is 3 you.' I'm deeply moved by a '56 feeling. Everyone's with us, it's just that the cavalry is late in arriving. In 1456, sixty thousand German and Polish crusaders reached Belgrade only several weeks after the battle.

'As children we are growing all the time. We grow a little bit bigger every day and every hour. We grow by such tiny bits that we don't notice it.

Yet we can see that we have grown.'* A scare story has been circulating in Belgrade that the lions in Sarajevo Zoo are being fed Serb children.

In craft classes, behind teacher's back, we carved swords and stakes, fired up by the Cold War. I was gobsmacked when the Red Indians ambushed us, the arrow lodged in my throat. I was a Yankee just once. They were already waiting for me at the János Hospital, complaining that I'd been neglecting them lately. After 1956 the sale of toy weapons was banned, lest we get too carried away, but home-made ones could be lethal. As a rule, the Russkies were the Red Indians and the Americans the cowboys, but sooner or later everybody got round to fighting everybody else. Nemes was given a die-cast machete, his father had been in North Vietnam. It came in handy during jungle warfare, but there weren't enough firearms. I nagged my dad into buying me a plastic pistol from the West. That was the break-through. I couldn't complain, though, we lacked for nothing: quartz watches, citrus fruit, Matchbox cars. My father missed out on promotions at work because he did not join the Party, but they needed his know-how and he got bonuses. My parents did not engage in political debates, they cursed the régime but did not fight it. They cursed me as well but did not fight me either; they judged the struggle would be hopeless.

Gillette, Gitanes, Geneva, genre, German, general, genocide, genius, gender, gesture, geometry, genetic engineer

For three hundred years the Turks exacted a 'blood levy' on children in the Balkans. Under this *devishirmeh* system, one boy in six was collected and then put through an intensive language course, religious education and military training in Istanbul. These janissaries lived in a permanent state of war, with any free time being devoted to Allah. In return, Allah guaranteed

unlimited career opportunities. The majority of the Ottoman grand viziers came from the ranks of Serbian, Croatian, Bosnian and Albanian children. The janissaries were the first standing army in Europe since the Romans: the *jenitsheri*, 'modern soldiery'. A cherry-picked army.

Graffito at the teachers training college: 'We love you, kids. From the paedophiles of Belgrade.'

h

három puszi = three kisses
háború = war
harag = anger
halál = death
hatalom = power
híradó = news bulletin
hazudnak = they're lying

Dad asked me to come by. They were knocking down the house in which I grew up to make room for a bigger and better one. On the train, I drank to the health of Hungarian girls with three mafiosi from Novi Sad. They would all have Hungarian wives, they said. I went to the Rudas Baths to melt away the Belgrade winter.

I stretched out in the light streaming in through the hexagonal holes in the vault, waiting to be shaken up like a snowstorm paperweight. The dome of the Rudas Baths is a continuation of the traveller's brow, a building which has holes by design, even without a siege — quintessential Budapest. I'm floating below the dome in an inverse snowfall, between hot water and a scorching sun: a Hungarian skull slipping into a Turkish helmet.

The next morning, I set out to pack up my childhood. The house is small, as if it were a model. The trees have shrunk: tiptoeing through a bonsai garden. The parental house stands empty, curtainless, with my room the only one still holding anything — packed with the Seventies, or to be more precise, from '75 to '85. Books and stones, photographs, love letters — I packed the lot into whisky boxes. I walked around the old villa. It only took a few seconds, I had outgrown the garden. There used to be a flight of steps under the old walnut tree, but that was covered with earth when the slope was taken into national ownership. A pharmacy was built where the orchard had once stood, a boiler house in the place of the apple trees. I stopped by the stone blocks that had once been used to carry palm-trees. The steps were several yards beneath me, in the ground. I lay down on the ground and rolled around until I was covered with snow.

I dreamt that we were frying spek, I got grease all over me. I climbed the walnut tree, but kept on slipping back down. I persevered until I had climbed all the trees. Children and trees of various sizes appear. They all grow together, leaves and branches, nails and hair, all the children were me and I climbed all the trees in the garden. Finally, I defied orders to get down, even though I knew the dream would end soon, so the children would not come down from the trees and the alarm clock goes off, the school bell rings, class starts, a tram clangs its bell, a ship blares its horn, a conductor blows his whistle and the bells of Belgrade toll — but the trees and children have all coalesced into one and they're laughing at me. I'm left standing down below, old and helpless, and up in every tree are children swinging their legs. That's how the dream ended, unfinished.

' "Can't get me, I've got pax!" — in hide-and-seek shouting this means that even if the seeker sees you, or the catcher catches you, it doesn't count.'*

War criminals must answer for their actions before the International Criminal Tribunal in The Hague. A war criminal is someone who enjoys what he does and in wartime acts in an uncivilized manner. He shoots from an off-side position, slops food on his opponents' clothes, never warns before attacking and always drops bombs on the sly.

The evening news on Serbian TV starts at seven-thirty. The news bulletin shows three protesters with flags and beer bottles who are sometimes Communists, sometimes Chetniks. I know them by sight. They're the three who've been demonstrating in Belgrade for the past forty days, and CNN is blowing it up like crazy. These three are responsible for all the disturbances, for misleading and alarming the populace of Belgrade. Milošević asserted to a foreign correspondent that it was Karadžić's men who were the rowdies on the streets of Belgrade. At seven-thirty those who don't like the régime start whistling and

* W–G, p. 43.

drumming. You get to know your neighbours. We stand at the window with wooden spoons and pans. I'm now in the process of splintering my fourth wooden spoon. For me, Belgrade is more the revolution of broken wooden spoons than of rotten eggs.

home, heroes, hussars, housewives, head-hunters, history, hide-and-seek, The Hague, hard of hearing, hawthorn, Habsburg, Hungarian, homesick

The late ninth century by the shore of Lake Balaton. There's a flat calm. You can hear the fish in the water; fat carp in the dense pondweed. Then all of a sudden, dust and hoof beats — the dust and hoof beats of a Magyar horseman beating a tactical retreat, Franks in hot pursuit. Dust and hoof beats, dust and hoof beats. Two Franks. An arrow is shot to the rear. One of the Franks clutches his heart. Once upon a time . . .

In shooting his arrow behind him, while conquering his future homeland, the valiant Magyar did not spot a pair of butterflies which crossed his path. Engaged in their nuptial dance, the butterflies were separated. One of them flew over Lake Balaton, lost its sense of direction and was done for. Its wings were soaked and its respiratory tubes became clogged. Anyone who has seen a butterfly thrashing on water is aware of the enthralling tension with which the air becomes charged in such moments. Through the vibrations set up by the thrashing wings, a town collapsed in India, burying thirty thousand people under the rubble; the English king, Alfred the Great, died; the Maya abandoned their ancient cities; the Bulgarians captured the White Castle that became Belgrade; the Vikings landed in Normandy; Abdurrahman, caliph of Cordoba, berated his gardener for a badly pruned rosebush; the Tang Dynasty collapsed in China; and in an Amerindian camp in the Amazon basin, the slave girl Dawn Light gave birth to quintuplets, which the cannibals took to be a good omen.

Roughly six hundred and sixty-six years later, the backwash of that butterfly's death throes created two empires on the shores of

Mehmed II the Conqueror seized two hundred cities and twelve countries. After capturing Byzantium, he overran the Balkans, but he got bogged down at Belgrade. According to one contemporary collection, the siege of Belgrade was inscribed on the majestic palimpsest of the Sultan's mind with the miraculous recording plume of his thought. This Ottoman graffito likened Belgrade to the very heavens and numbered its weapons as multitudinous as the stars. But the licentious, filthy and gluttonous Magyars provoked the patient Sultan into attacking. As an illustration of the situation, a miniature was painted which showed Mehmed chopping off Hunyadi's head. A hand-painted propaganda codex.

There is a picture of the Hungarian and Turkish presidents shaking hands in the Belgrade Room of Hungary's Parliament building. They have identical grins and identically bald pates. On the walls, scenes of mortal combat. According to my Turkish friends, our two peoples have been fused in the grand crucible of history: we've become part Turkish, they, part Hungarian. That may explain why the shackled Turkish prisoners and the Franciscan monks standing in the foreground are all bald. Only Hunyadi's hair is flapping in the wind. But then, wasn't he Romanian?

The seven points of the Hunyadi 'DIY Hero' kit:
1. Anyone who is born will die.
2. No-one is born a hero.
3. A hero is born when he dies.

Lake Balaton, one to the north, one to the south. In one the sun never set; in the other, it was always rising. The border sundered the Hungarians, who thus became their own neighbours: two Hungarian provinces with Hungarian governments and with Hungarian populaces paying taxes to both sides, Habsburgs and Ottomans. The Ottoman Empire stretched from Aden to Algiers, from Basra to Buda and the Balaton; the Habsburg possessions stretched from Košice to Cuzco, from Tenochtitlán to Tokay, with the Balaton at their border. That is how, at the end of the Middle Ages and the dawn of the Modern Age, the Hungarians found themselves in one and the same empire as Incas and Persians. The Balaton was a common territorial water, with prowling gunboat patrols, both linking and dividing the two worlds, from the Mayas to the Copts, from the Pacific to the Indian Ocean. Waves have been breaking on the Balaton ever since. It's no coincidence that the country's only decent tectonic fault line is situated here. Let that suffice to show how rash and risky it is to shoot arrows to the rear. That'll teach the Magyars to mind their manners.

4. A hero dies while carrying out his mission.
5. It is a tragic lapse for a hero's death to be postponed, necessitating the hero's downfall.
6. One is either a hero or not a hero.
7. No-one lives for ever.

'Our hair is constantly growing. By about this much every month: ←1cm→. On a piece of scalp this big (see right) there are about two hundred strands of hair.'*

The demo for the dictatorship began with ten thousand posters of Slobodan Milošević being handed out. The bashful dictator's arsenal of mimicry and the stations of his hair loss can be traced on historical snapshots. The twenty-fold enlargements of his passport photos indicate the bearings of his supporters. The North is benevolent and paternal, yet not suave; the East is strict, yet understanding, not expecting unnecessary sacrifices; the South is steely and implacable, a victorious military leader marching at the head of his troops; while the West is a dreamy dickhead caught off guard by the photographer, lips puckered as if blowing a kiss. The salient quiff of hair on the crown of his head gives the distinct impression of a glans. Oil and watercolour paintings that are being carried around by a creative group among the sauntering throng like a travelling exhibition are testaments to the nexus of authority and coiffure. Artists who have accepted the iconographic consistency of baldness have created uniquely personal pieces that depict the man as a political animal in lyrical tones. The perpetual shifting of the images is part and parcel of the spatiotemporal enjoyment of the portraits. A viewer has to work for his artistic pleasure, unlike in the traditional museum space, where his gaze would quickly slide past, leaving the hapless artwork, in all its stationariness, to fend for itself. The pictures do not depend on the rigid lines of a wall or museum room but fit organically into the totality of the street and the demonstration. The viewer must pursue the picture, jumping up and down among heads, avoiding placards, thus becoming subsumed into the group. The cyclic motion of the pictures is an avant-garde gesture that adumbrates early cinematography — a sign to the recipient that the pictures per se cannot represent a subject for analysis, but they need to be considered as collectively forming a composition. In this manner, the Venus de Milo and Milo Muppet communicate with a gigantic image of a Gargling Milošević that bears a hair-raising resemblance to Kojak, interacting with a petty-realistic charm that belies the mundane realities of war.

Belgrade, 1456: heat wave and pestilence. Mehmed's ships have been sunk, his cannon turned against him, his troops massacred. The Crusaders spend four days tossing the corpses of the besieging army into the Danube. According to a farsighted Turkish source, the bride of victory revealed her face in the mirror of procrastination.

'Budapest lies to the north of Mohács.'**

Nationalistic Serbs reckon this is where world wars begin. Two have already started on Serbia's

* W–G, p. 61.
** W–G, p. 44.

account, so quake in your boots, USA! They shake their fists, having failed to notice that they've lost the war. The inhabitants of Belgrade think they have moved into the focal point of history, with the eyes of the world upon them, in other words, they are bound to win.

'The body, which had a head, was sought by the leg. The head, which had a body, shouted woe is me, and the one in whose body the soul was still present, but to no avail, sought death from the god of fate.'*

When medieval Hungary foundered, Buda and Baghdad, the Dead Sea and Lake Balaton became part of the same country. The dizzying prospects of a new Europe, extending from the Carpathians to California, sprang up on the ruins of the disintegrating kingdom. The dry-land frontiers of two empires wound their way through Hungary, nine hundred miles from the Adriatic to Satu Mare, one castle every five miles, a medieval Stone Curtain, on either side of which were Hungarians who believed they were at the focal point of world history when the forces of Good and Evil were clashing. The Hungarians saw the advancing Turks as the agents of Doomsday, visited on them by God because of their sins. They thought the end of the world had come. It was not the world that came to an end, however, just the Middle Ages. In the Middle Ages the Hungarians believed everything would end; when I was a child, they believed nothing would ever end.

Two housewives catch each other's eye at the demonstration. It is the first time they have seen one other. They are wearing similar clothes. One is waving from the window, the other is marching with her husband. A couple of days later they come face to face on the street: same smile, same hat. They now read the opposition papers together, they are friends.

'When the day's teaching is done I go home. I live near school and I soon get home. My mother also comes home early.

Homeward bound, all the way,
the thought I hold to most strong
is how I shall greet Mother,
whom I haven't seen for so long.

Hungary is my home. A Soviet child's home is the Soviet Union.'**

i

idő van = time's up
igazság = truth
igen = yes

In the film *Independence Day* extraterrestrial beings launch an attack on the Earth to kill off all life — human, animal and plant. This is

explicitly admitted by a captured extraterrestrial through the medium of a dead earthling's larynx. In the first third of the film the aliens, who enjoy absolute technical superiority, destroy all of the Earth's big cities. The scene in which the

---

*   Legend to a battle scene in a Turkish miniature, Topkapi Seray Museum, Hazine 1517.
** W–G, p. 65.

White House is atomized receives storms of applause in Belgrade cinemas. An audience member wearing a baseball cap dances up to the screen, shaking his fist and slapping his thighs American-style: *Yeh! Yeh! Yeh!*

'The opposite of yes is no.'*

information, inflation, invasion, independence, innocence, inheritance, intelligence, invisible, indigo, infidel, infarct, inquisition, intuition, intensive care

The students stood accused, with the TV saying they weren't students at all. The next day they set off for the demonstrations with their school record books in hand. Students waving little red books flooded the streets. A sense of *déjà vu*, back to Peking in '66 and Paris in '68, only this time in Tinseltown technicolour. Would you know you were at the battle of Hastings if all you'd seen was the Bayeux Tapestry? The students come along with little red books. At first glance they're Maoists, but if you look closer, they are holding crosses and icons in their shivering hands. I see a 'Better dead than red' badge. I remove the *ushanka* from my head. 'We're taking the opposite direction to right,' say the pacemakers as they come up to a bend in the road. They can't articulate which way that would be. Shouting football slogans is fair enough, most of them are Red Star Belgrade fans anyway. It's all become a bit of a dog's breakfast, a post-modern demo.

I put the *ushanka*, with its ear flaps, back on, it's cold and the cops are coming, jaws all lined up.

The demolition of our house was postponed. My father had a heart attack at the age of fifty-six. That's how old his own father had been when he was born. His hair turned grey in the ICU, and we didn't even notice. We kept tapping the heart machine and joking with the nurses. He was connected to a TV monitor, picture and sound, with three plugs, like in a video game: a live transmission from the heart. The hospital ward enveloped the sleeping patients like a snowy landscape. White walls, white beds, white bedside cabinets, white blankets — but above the door an unequivocally black clock with a heart-shaped second hand. Pedagogy or a sense of humour? We were weighing up the chances of someone laughing themselves to death when the nurse came in. Her name was Angie. Would I be so good as to go. My father was the best thing in the old régime. I dedicate this book to him. He lived under real existing socialism as if it did not exist. He brought up his sons in conformity with the virtues of the age of chivalry. They were fond of him. They may have laughed at him, but they never doubted his sincerity. He was an inventor, but he could not earn enough from that to support his family, and so he became a businessman, which he knew nothing about. He loved working and called business meetings conversations. He would say he'd just been to a conversation, it had been most interesting, and then he would tell us that he'd sold a software package — some-

thing with which he was as familiar as an Arab with his camel. My father, the expert. He wrote a book about magnetic data media. He had such a childish trust in success that I felt like a grown-up by his side. I still feel like a grown-up next to my father, and no-one makes me cry more heartily. His pulse was fifty-six, his blood pressure 100/56. Pedagogy or a sense of humour?

Belgraders say that the inflation of the dinar during the embargo hit a world-record high mark. If you were casual about getting to the shops, your money could lose half its value. In the pedestrian precinct homeless people have their picture taken clothed in dinar bills of nine-digit denominations. I got into a heated argument in defence of Hungary holding the record. In the Hungarian hyperinflation of late 1945–early '46 the fall in value of the pengő went at least ten zeroes higher than the dinar. The Serbs like to brag about their records: inflation, the suicide rate, alcohol consumption. It's so Balkan! Over white wine, using inflationary dinars as coasters, we joke about the hypothetical dinar values of Serb Romantic poets:

Vuk Karadžić	10,000
Petar Njegoš	50,000
J.J. Zmaj	500,000
Đura Jakšić	5,000,000,000.

Í

ítéletidő = dirty weather
íratlan törvények = unwritten rules
ígéretek = promises
író = writer

Dirty weather. December, snow, subzero temperatures, icicles on beards. Someone has to go, the cold needs to be chased away to make room for spring. Strike up the fifes and drums and rattles, it's Mardi Gras in Mohács. We're off to protest, to make a din with anything we can — fifes and drums, reed fiddles and bells, key bunches and Coca-Cola cans, censers and chandeliers,

Very ugly

fifth offensive, the rings came rolling off the fingers of the partisans. They were so ravenous that they chewed the bark from trees. Nevertheless, they broke through and won the war. What could he have known about letters that scared him so much?

flags and icons, flashlights and loo-seats, nappies and evening newspapers, eggs and tomatoes, ocarinas and triangles, bagpipes and trumpets, gongs and silver trays, ladles and tuning forks, pots and wooden spoons, bricks and rattles, mouths . . .

irony, ivory, identity, ISBN, isolate, irate, iron curtain, poison ivy

Richard Burton and Elizabeth Taylor played Marshal Tito in the film *Hammersmith is Out, Sutjeska* in 1972. Liz wasn't actually in the picture, but during the shoot Tito invited the couple to his summer dacha. *Sutjeska* is about the fifth German offensive, when the united German, Italian and Croat forces tried to wipe the partisans off the map. The decisive battle claimed untold casualties, with neither side taking prisoners. The actor who played Šurda was also in the film, he takes out three tanks with a bazooka. During the shoot Tito told Burton that he had never signed any execution orders — not because he was afraid of being held responsible, oh no, he was the boss, after all. It was the written word he feared, his own handwriting — that the letters might turn against him. He even dictated his autobiography, subsequently amending it, during the Seventies, only in TV interviews. Tito, witness to the century, he grew up in the Austro-Hungarian Monarchy, fought in both World Wars, saw the purges in Moscow, and was personally acquainted with all the great dictators of the twentieth century. Churchill received a Nobel Prize for his memoirs, Tito left nothing for posterity. During the

j

javak = goods
játék = game
jaj = Ouch!
Jugó = Yugo

His gravestone was inscribed with the codename he had been given in the Movement, as with other great men. The name Tito stuck while he was in the underground resistance: it was borrowed from an eighteenth-century Croatian writer. Originally he had wanted Rudi, but there was already a Comrade Rudi, so he had to find another alias. When he was liaising with Moscow he also went by the name Walter. Even after the war, Stalin regularly Waltered Tito when he wanted to get him going, as was indeed his wont. Josef and Josip — two Joes, two models. In 1917 Stalin is supposed to have held up a train on the railway line that Tito had helped build as a POW. It might even be true.

The open-air festivities of Belgrade had the following programme: a mass demonstration with half a million extras, a beauty contest for riot

35

cops, snowball tossing over the cordon, volley-ball with rotten fruit, chess, footie, hide-and-seek, tag, drive-thru demos, midnight parades, sheep herding, blockades by broken-down cars, crowd dispersal with tear gas, rubber truncheons or water cannons, jail walks by students in prison garb, evening classes for the cops, theatre performances, fancy-dress parades, air raids with paper planes, condoms and toilet rolls, beatings-up of opposition leaders, lynchings. Many other events were down to pure chance.

Yugoslav air stewardess Vesna Vuletić fell thirty-three thousand three hundred and thirty feet for the sake of alliteration (*Guinness Book of Records*) to break the previous free-fall record, held by Russian pilot I. M. Chisov, who was shot down by the Luftwaffe in 1942 from a height of two thousand three hundred and sixty three feet. Vesna Vuletić came to after being in a coma for twenty-seven days, Lieutenant Chisov managed to crawl to a nearby village before losing consciousness. On the other hand, he fell on his backside, in deep snow.

'Games are for amusement. Grown-ups play games too. I can be whatever I want for fun: a diver, a schoolteacher, even an astronaut. The carpet can be the sea and the armchair a spaceship. I can make cakes from sand, though I wouldn't dream of eating them, of course!'*

Redistribution of goods. Riot cops are paid four times as much as university lecturers. The police cost the Milošević administration one million Deutschmarks a day. Not everyone can be a riot cop, there isn't enough money — the wealth has to be redistributed.

Ouch! They're beating up a cameraman, who is shielding the camera with his body. He cries in surprise, and is even more surprised by his own voice. He yells into the mike. He can see himself on the monitor, which gives him strength.

* W–G, p. 73.

He's on air right now, not yet a victim. He might even become a hero and strike back, the picture and sound are all his own work. Ow-oo-ow! The second ouch recalls the first: he's afraid of the next blow, because he knows there will be a next blow. He's not paying attention to himself any more but to the truncheon, he's learning what pain is. Ouch! he's learning fear. Ouch! he's afraid. By the third ouch he's a pro. He's found his voice, that of suffering. He gives up the fight, sets his camera aside and starts begging. Ouch! Don't hurt me!

jaywalk, jungle, jail, jaws, jazz, jewelry, Janissary, jabberwocky, Joseph, joy

Yugo, a fantasy name for: (a) a four-piece kitchen suite; (b) a twentieth-century country; (c) wooden building blocks. Only one answer is correct. The prevailing ideological current of the Fifties considered the Yugoslavian way to be a reform of the Soviet model, which, being a liberalized version, would result in a welfare state. After a visit to Kim Il Sung, though, Tito sided once and for all with the counter-reformation. He was mesmerized by the idea of eternity.

* W–G, p. 68.

'Snow is frozen water vapour. It falls from clouds in soft, white flakes. It turns into water when it melts. Snowflakes are star-shaped.'*

k

karnevál = carnival
katona = soldier
köd = fog
k. u. k. (kaiserliche und königliche) = Kakanian (Imperial and Royal)
kontramíting = counter-demo

Josip Broz was born on 7 May 1892 in Varaždin County, Croatia. He was the seventh child in the family, one of seven who survived into adolescence. From the age of seven he worked on his father's land, at fourteen he became a mechanic's apprentice and at the age of twenty-one he was called up by the Kakanian army. Including time spent as a POW, Josip was a soldier for seven years. He spent the same number of years in jail or under detention. He became a partisan leader at the age of forty-nine (7×7). Seven years later,

Yugoslavia severed relations with the Soviet Union. He was seventy-seven years old when the author of this *Window–Giraffe* was conceived.

'Seven is a number. I write it so: 7. 7 days is one week. 7 is one more than 6. The dragon in fairy-tales has seven heads. If we did not know it only exists in fairy-tales, we would be afraid of it.'*

When he was seven years old, Tito told the priest that the mass was boring. The priest ticked him off: You're a bad lad. From that time on, Tito did not believe in badness. Kumrovec, Tito's native village, lies on the banks of the River Sutla, on the border between historical Austria and Hungary. On the first page of his autobiography he mentions that towering over Kumrovec was the ghost of Barbara Erdődy, who was going to carry him off to Tsarograd Castle if he did not go to sleep like a good boy. His mother used the ghost of Countess Erdődy to scare little Tito, who tried to get his revenge by day with his wooden sword at the foot of the castle. Ten years later he was runner-up at the *k.u.k.* fencing championship in Budapest.

The Broz family were bondservants, property of the Erdődys, and in Tito's imagination they fought with Máté Gubec against Ferenc

Tahy in the Croatian serf uprising of 1572. Tahy had been a comrade-in-arms of Count Zrínyi, the hero of Szigetvár in 1566, but he survived the siege. The odds of surviving the insurrection were much rosier than at Szigetvár, but in Tito's imagination hundreds of serfs hung from the trees he had climbed as a child in the surrounding countryside. After the war, Krsto Hegedušić's painting of the battle took pride of place in Tito's office as a symbol of the fight against oppression. In a recent film, Tito emerges from his mausoleum and stops to chat with the people of Belgrade. They accuse him of having died too soon and not giving Milošević enough power.

The official organs set the day of the counter-demo for 24 December. Santa Claus bussed in protesters from the countryside all around. Fifty thousand new faces to grace the season of goodwill. The socialist 'Spartakiads' of old were resuscitated, with the delegates marching to Belgrade Castle

* W–G, pp. 67 & 112.

with sodding great signs. But try as they might to find the main square, Milošević's supporters lost their way in the strange city. They broke up into smaller groups and scrutinized the shoppers with undisguised mistrust, as if expecting them to turn into an anti-régime rabble at any moment. Milošević felt that television had gone too far. It was going too far when the evening news called the opposition's demonstrations fascist. It was also going too far when a pro-government demonstrator shot down one of Vuk Drašković's supporters on the street in broad daylight. But it was really going too far when an opposition protester was battered to death with police help. Predrag Starčević, the only fatality of the demonstrations, was alleged to have been deliberately driven around the city until he died of his wounds. After that, the cops marched out in force to defend the contras. The counter-demonstrators were pelted with eggs and potatoes hurled over the heads of the police, while they responded by throwing back their placards. Snowballs came flying from both

directions, occasionally hitting a cop. Milošević made a speech in which he censured the ranters who were out to destroy the country and Western agitators, who were everywhere. The crowd, moved to tears, demanded Vuk's arrest, but their leader turned a deaf ear. In the end, the fifty thousand–strong 'contra' claque proclaimed their love in chorus, at which the dictator, in his embarrassment, forgot himself: *I love you too*, the loudspeakers sighed, barely audibly.

'To say a person is two-faced does not mean he has two faces, just that he is acting as if he were something other than he is.'*

Radovan Karadžić, poet, politician, psychiatrist, psychopath, war criminal. The secrets of the soul are familiar to him, even his critics concede he is the greatest of all psychiatrist poets. Especially recommended is his volume *Split Personality* and a piece starting 'Going to town to beat up the scum'. In a poem written fifteen years earlier, he predicted the destruction of Sarajevo, which he later orchestrated in person. It is still an open question whether that self-fulfilling prophecy of this multitalented creator should be regarded as part of his literary or medical oeuvre. Is it the confession of a

* W–G, p. 80.

mouth gaping, like in the movies. Photographers are swarming all around her, an eager, international crew. We could be anywhere, except we're not. Were King Kong to come along, he would carry Dunja off to the top of the Empire State Building or the towers of the Hotel Moscow, with Belgrade at Dunja's feet, and the world would be goggling at that, the sky, not the cops, and lines would be drawn around the clouds. That would be nice, to trace lines around every woman.

prophet who is struggling to understand the world, or of a Dr. Jekyll who is attempting a cure? During the war in Bosnia, a correspondent asked the doctor where he obtained the fuel for his tanks if he was not supported by Yugoslavia. Karadžić admitted that his soldiers had come across German depots from the Second World War hidden in a cave. Perhaps a hundred years from now someone will be struck by a fresco in Greater Serbia's Parliament showing the poet as he strikes oil from the rocks of Herzegovina.

An outline is being traced around the girl. She is sprawled on the ground, blushing and grinning as if she were alive. Stop laughing, you're supposed to be dead. The asphalt is cold and the chalk keeps snapping. They're trying to reconstruct the crime, but it's not easy, because she can't stop laughing. Because it tickles. Good job she didn't put on a skirt — that would have been real fun! Nobody thought to tell her what to wear, numbskulls. They are busy reconstructing the crime, re-enacting the events. Who did what to whom, and how. Body pitted against body. She ought to be kicked now, for real, then beaten over the head with a rubber truncheon. Now faint, Dunja, all right? And Dunja faints,

drawn around the clouds. That would be nice, to trace lines around every woman.

'A cloudless sky is blue in colour.'*

A minister drives into the crowd, nearly running the people over as they are re-enacting the crime. The Commissar for Refugee Affairs tries to break through the throng but is surrounded by people who spit on his car. They start drawing a line around him. The re-enactment of the crime continues. Tito relates how in the Austro-Hungarian army they used to pull the legs of new recruits by sending them off to catch a frog, then get them to draw a chalk line round it and watch that it didn't leap out of the circle. After straining for a while to mesmerize the frog into staying put, the new recruit would be left pursing his lips at the very least.

A tearful officer asks us to disperse, half into the loudspeaker, half into his walkie-talkie. Please

This is what light blue looks like   This is what dark blue looks like   This is what purple looks like

---

*   W–G, p. 68; for more on clouds, see p. 76.

disperse, he says. Disperse yourself, an elderly lady retorts. She's sixtyish and is wearing a paper hat with the words 'I'm just an innocent bystander.' We will not be dispersed any more. We have a good tail-wind, the sun is shining in the policemen's eyes. Time is on our side.

Hungarian TV comes towards us, filming me as a Belgrade student. On the thirtieth day of demonstrations, the mood is unbowed, our correspondent reports from the Danube-Tisza-Drava-Sava interfluve. In Belgrade, they're bombarding the High Court building with condoms.

You can learn lots of interesting things about Belgrade from this dictionary. Read more about the jungle on p. 73.

Kaiser, kosher, kosmos, KO, keyhole, kremlin, koan, kisser, killer, kingdom come, Kakanian kamikaze

After Milošević's Christmas address, the demonstrators stand in front of the riot cops with cardboard shields bearing the words 'I love you, too.' The cops chat amiably with old partisans, joke with

students, show girls their gas masks. Five minutes later they send them running in all directions: an order had come over the radio. An invisible hand twirls a rubber truncheon, pressing my head against the wall.* Then, just as suddenly the cordon melts away. There's no knowing if they're heading somewhere else, or just that the daily allowance has run out, since they are paid by the hour. The cops stop us, then let us pass, but two streets further on they form another line, though this too lasts only a couple of hours before they finally leave, with the civilians giving them the finger to help them on their way. Towards evening, the Terazije is once again blocked by multiple cordons. Belgrade is holding itself back. The cordon has some play, slipping a few hundred yards this way and that. Months of petting, and just one fatality. It is repeatedly being pulled down, there is nothing permanent or irrevocable about it. The set keeps changing, the props get broken or are replaced, no two performances are alike. Everybody is actor and audience in one. Due to the size of the stage, no-one can take in the entire show, only excerpts — a never-ending dress rehearsal of a work-in-progress, a revolution which never reaches its dramatic climax, constant suppression, delayed ejaculation, a city on the verge of orgasm. On the brink of exhaustion and

---

* 'Anything we press against something else will leave its mark.' W–G, p. 108.

euphoria. Belgrade is at the heart of the country, where the dividing lines meet. Students and police, Europe and the Balkans, street and theatre, Danube and Sava, eclecticism and modernism, the Monarchy looking the Turk unflinchingly in the eye.

By way of a side street, a group of students dodges the cordon and pops up on the other side. Infantile capering, comic-strip wheezes: Dumb cops, you won't catch me! Reinforcements arrive and the students begin to play tag with the riot police, showing up unexpectedly at various points in town, with radio broadcasting a running commentary. The riot cops' uniform is ill suited to pursuing students: the shields joggle up and down, sticks slap against thighs. The hard core of demonstrators melts away, then pops up again on Slavia Square. The cops are regrouped, setting up a trap in the nearby streets, but the demonstrators who are on the run are swallowed up by the Earth. Anxious moments of waiting. No news. The cops are about to move on.

'Who's gonna wash away all this shit?' the newspaper woman yells as she sweeps fifty scrambled eggs towards the garbage can. The students want to beat her up, but Vuk comes to her rescue. Violence will lead nowhere, for all that he wants to lead. Vuk says he understands them: he too was a rebel once, a '68-er. He and his friends took part in demos for fewer cars and more hospitals. Then, in the Seventies, he was the Tanjug news agency's war correspondent in Africa, but he lost his job when he reported on a war that hadn't even started yet. He could not wait. Vuk is an icon personified. He's protesting as if he were already looking back from the other side, as if they might come for him at any moment — the angels or the secret police. For now, though, he's here and enjoining us to lighten up. Stuff that, the newspaper lady yells back at him. I suppose you're gonna sweep this shit up! The smile does not melt on Vuk's face.

/

Everyone thinks they've given up when the radio announces that the action group has gone on to the railway station. The senior officer civilly asks us to leave the square. A young, moustachioed cop behind us whispers to the girls: Please don't stop now! He squeezes my hand by mistake.

'Anything we do not know but would like to know, we ask about. We get an answer to the question.'*

lábak = legs
lányok = girls
lerobban = break down
legszebb = fairest
lehallgatnak = you're under surveillance

We drive into the city centre and break down on Avenue of the Revolution. The car engine stalls in front of Parliament, of all places. There's a line several miles long of cars with their hoods up. Passengers and drivers are walking around,

* W–G, p. 80.

Lynching is in the air. And we're the ones they're out to lynch. Truncheons are flashed, scattering the fog into small patches of mist. It's time to ask myself what I'm doing. In whose place am I standing here, and whose head are they trying to smash in?

'I got up early today. This is a sentence. I put a full stop at its end. When I ask a question, I put a question mark at the end of the sentence, like this: "What time is it?" If I say "Come here, Péter!" I put an exclamation mark at the end of the sentence.' *

language, languish, label, labour, lace, laid, liar, liver, list, legs, lexicon, long, loose, loo, love, limbo, literature, last word

I'm being bugged, just like in the good old days. A sign has been put up: This room is subject to surveillance! My heart beats faster. They still care if I'm against them. To sit down to work in this room. To search for bugs, like looking for your lover's erogenous zones. To whisper sweet nothings in the ears of the secret police, hiding the silence in empty suitcases. At the university press office they're eavesdropping on the buggers, while we, for our part, form a cordon in front of the police cordon. The protesters are alike in being different, the cops are different in being alike. They have uniform.

The Belgraders gather under the flags of various nations, multiethnic brands and subcultures: Brazilian, Canadian, French, Italian, Ferrari, Fiorentina, Ayrton Senna, Bob Marley, Coca-Cola. Their word for a flag is 'zastava' — same as the car model. 'The flag is streaming in the wind. For that reason, it is sometimes also called a streamer.

shaking their heads. The damn thing, it's shot, thanks to the spare-parts shortage caused by the embargo. A man in a general's uniform is strutting up and down with a stethoscope round his neck. He bends over the engine with a frown: that's what it is, he says. Ticker trouble. We abandon the car and walk all along the line. A minibus has shed a wheel, a truck ran out of fuel right in front of the Opera, a Zastava's steering wheel is wobbling — it's just one of those days when everything goes wrong. The cops start a fight and remove a Reliant Robin from the intersection, the disabled driver inside gesticulating wildly. Everything is falling apart: fan belts snap, gear sticks won't engage, a trolleybus's collecting pole has come off the overhead cable.

* W–G, p. 101.

Hey, glorious winds are setting our flag streaming, inscribed upon it the slogan: Long live liberty!*

Like English loos, the cordon is kinder to women. The chicks rate the cops by their moustaches and how long it takes them to make them blush. The blushing time is inversely proportional to the thickness of the moustache. But where are the policewomen? Vivacious police kittens, winking from under their helmets; pleasingly plump, motherly lady cops, fuzz-mommies who drag you home by the ear; immaculate, braided *Polizeifraus*; black-belt police peaches, high-booted babes with rapid-fire asses — Where are you? Where, oh where?

Eris tossed an apple earmarked 'for the fairest' amidst the wedding banquet guests. That was how the Trojan War began. The golden apple is a symbol of the sun and of immortality. Paris awarded it to Aphrodite, goddess of love, in exchange for the most beautiful woman in the world, her earthly counterpart, which is to be understood metaphorically. Some believed that Aphrodite gave the apple to her lover as a pledge, since she was immortal already.

The golden apples were tended by the Hesperides in a garden in the far west, where the sun disappears into the ocean, which is why at sunset the sky is like a tree bent under the weight of its fruit. The orchard lies on the borderline of life and death, or to be more precise, on the borderline of death and immortality. When the horizon splits the sun into half of a dark-red apple, the goddess's star, Venus, rises in the sky.

The tree was guarded by a many-headed dragon who spoke many tongues. In Christianity everything was stood on its head: the dragon was metamorphosed from interpreter into seducer, knowledge became sin, and the lovers relinquished their immortality in exchange for the apple. Adam and Eve pass through the gate going the other way, into the land of death and suffering, but in a sliced apple one can still find the goddess's five-pointed star, which for freemasons is a sign of the spirit hidden inside matter. In the Middle Ages, the golden apple was the privilege of kings. Snow White was brought back from clinical death by the love of a prince. Prince Argelus finds himself a bride among

the fairies with the help of a golden apple. For the Turks, too, the apple tree stands on the western border as a metaphor for the most recently conquered city and for power over the whole world. Through an explosive demographic transition, the garden becomes a city, and in the writings of Ottoman authors the apple crops up in the guise of Rome, Vienna, and Cologne. The apple reappears in modern mythology as a vehicle of knowledge. King Matthias presented his smartest page with a coat of arms incorporating a golden apple. Newton hit on the theory of gravitation after seeing a falling apple.

At our high school the students helped out with the apple harvest. We picked Golden Delicious by Lake Balaton for export to the West. I used to imagine people 'over there'

*   W–G, pp. 92 & 157.

chomping the apples I'd gathered. Golden worms. They call New York the Big Apple. Milošević's people tried to drive the opposition out of the city with apples. Handing out apples to the pro-government demonstrators was a post-modern gesture. As a striking response to the theatricality of the anti-Communist protests, the mass brawl on 24 December began as an apple-throwing contest. The Belgrade populace, having no apples, beat off the ideological attack with eggs, spuds, and rotten veg.

Eris's sacred tree was the thorn-apple. The stake used to pierce the heart of a vampire should be carved from the wood of a thorn-apple. A vampire hunts for the fairest of them all, and that is why it cannot die.

Bram Stoker, the author of *Dracula*, relied for his low-down on vampires on an exotically-named Hungarian orientalist friend. Arminius Vámbéry relayed to him data on the habits of the bloodsuckers of the Carpathian Basin, though he personally thought the whole thing pretty silly.

Good feet are hard to find. Feet get worn out, run ragged. In Belgrade, the square fills up with feet every day. On New Year's Day one million feet stand in front of the National Museum carrying you along, heads bobbing up and down in synch, like in a swimming pool with a wave machine. One million feet treading on my toes. The square is full to bursting, there is no room for more feet — not

on the ground, anyway. I trundle ahead on a carpet of toes. Feet beneath me, feet above, but I carry on as if wading through dough. I can't keep it up for long, however. The crowd presses me against a wall, the wall also has a face. The band strikes up, people stand on my shoulders, children are hoisted high above heads. A woman faints and is passed through a ground-floor window. One of my hands is stuck in my pocket, I can't pull it out, I help with my head. We step in chorus, scream in chorus, sing in chorus. At midnight I crash through the surface, and in a state of weightlessness clink glasses with my neighbours. The crowd hoists me up onto a nearby balcony to be hugged and kissed: Happy New Year! I soar up, up, and away, like the bubbles in champagne. Belgrade, 1997: learn to float!

'The day after today, every day, is tomorrow.'*

---

* W–G, p. 68.

ly

lyuk = hole

In 1956, the quincentenary of Hunyadi's triumphant defence of Belgrade, Budapest was blown to bits. Pressing new venues into service, the Soviet army revived the traditions of the siege of '44. The city is riddled with holes: holes on house walls, holes between houses, new holes mixed up with old. Whether a house looks the way it does due to the siege or the revolution, because of '44 or '56, used to be a constant subject of debate: It can't be '44, it's a new building! The hell it is — typical Bauhaus! Can't you see the curved terrace? Then the snow would fall and cover up all the holes. Then more snow would fall, and the new snow got mixed up with the old, so one could no longer tell which

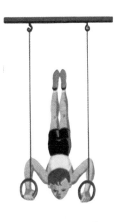

snow was covering up all those holes, and people waited for the snow to melt, because the country was in the grip of eternal snow. Forty thousand big and several million smaller holes. Budapest is the city of holes. I was born in this city of holes, with bullet holes on its hospital walls, holey gravestones. A seven-foot grass snake slithered into the crypt of Baron Manó Schwanbergi Kruchina (and his wife Marianne) before my very eyes. The baron died in '56, his wife in '44. A victim of the class struggle, or a drunken monumental mason? The gravestone later disappeared, leaving a hole in its place. Then a new grave came to replace the hole — a hole cycle could be traced in that way. The house in which we lived had been built on the hole left by my grandfather's house. As a child my father used to play in bomb craters in the garden. The bigger holes had houses built on them, smaller ones were used as rubbish dumps. Discarded TV sets and radio valves lay in heaps at the back of the garden, an electronic junk yard on Liberty Hill. In one hole we found a winged bomb, and even that had a hole in it, someone had screwed off the detonator head. We climbed walls, stuck our fingers into the holes and with our eyes shut tried to imagine the bullets. A Braille modern history of Budapest — a city that cannot be seen by the eye, only felt with fingers, read between the lines: house-wall-sized hieroglyphs, epic and lyric

madarak = birds
magyarok = Hungarians
magyaráz = explain
minden = everything
mellek = breasts
mi = we

variations, wartime graffiti, crude erotic messages, an inside-out archive.

Even today Budapest lives off holes. The city's new demands are creating new holes, gaps that spring up overnight, sites large enough to feature on maps, and to have office blocks crammed into them. Right now, Russian mafiosi are blowing holes, big and small, into the body of the city. The feel of the holes has changed, however. The days of a Nineties hole are numbered, it's hardly been dug before it's filled in. Where are the enduring old pocks made by nine-millimetre shells, the respectable dints of 23-mm rounds, the loud-mouthed hollows of 38-mm or the eye-watering cavities of 85-mm shells? The holes of yesteryear.

It was useless sticking my finger in holes in the walls of Osijek and Vukovar, the thrill had gone. The buildings were just like those in any small Hungarian town, but the holes felt strange — as if houses had been shot up, not people, frustrations being vented on walls, with the bullets still lodged in the holes. There were no great causes here, no heroes born, just plaster angels left over from the Austro-Hungarian Monarchy and shot through the forehead in a macho aesthetic of wanton destruction. Heading south, a Karadžić poster on a road sign: 'The man who did not betray us'.

The historic building on top of Eagle Hill where I went to school had been a convent before it was upgraded into an institution of learning. When German troops occupied Hungary, in March 1944, they set up their HQ in the main hall. This is where Budapest's military commander was detained. The hall later served as our gym, and we ran round and round in circles between its historic walls, a domestic history in a tucked handstand. The Magyars entered Hungary along the highway of nations, said our walrus-moustached PE instructor, which sounded good. I could just imagine them trying to hitch a lift on the steppes, holding up a marrowbone with 'Hungary' scratched on it in runic script, but nobody could read it. Leapfrog over the box and a cartwheel on landing. According to sir, a huge expanse of wasteland stretches from the Pacific to the Great Hungarian Plain, roughly from the Amur to the Danube, with the Magyars at one end and the Gulag at the other, so we'd better behave. He dished out two-handed slaps so we would not lose our balance — his idea of the golden mean. I would rather have climbed a pole or done two circuits. No more helping hands, he said, and bore down on me with all the gravitas he could muster. He just wanted to mould me into *an upright Hungarian*. Something didn't add up, because although our language was supposed to be our greatest remaining treasure, they were trying to get me to hold my tongue. Domestic history merged into anatomy, patriotism into grammar, solidarity into moulding. To cut a long story short, the Magyars came to Hungary a thousand years ago, and they've kept on coming ever since. No-one knows where

from or where to, and anyone who says differently is wrong, or not Magyar, or not honest. The Magyars are shrouded in mystery, or lost. The Magyars do not stand out: they look just like anybody else and assimilate with ease wherever they may be, except in Hungary, where they are divided by a common tongue. The Magyar has a little bit of the Serbo-Croat in him, a little bit homeless. He marches down the highway of nations, driving huge herds of cattle before him, and is constantly at war. Gusts of wind sneak up behind him to deliver gigantic slaps in the face. No messing about here! My own image of the Magyars combined the progressive traditions of the Wild West and the Wild East, growing out of a close study of Karl May's stories and Árpád Feszty's panorama of the *Magyars Entering Hungary*, now on view in the Ópusztaszer National Memorial Park. The Magyars lived like cowboys, and fought like Red Indians. They collected antiquities long before the great explorers. Cortés and Pizarro are descendants of the Magyar leaders Lehel and Bulcsú. The Magyar Indians raided the Middle Ages, holding them up halfway like some stagecoach, circling them, whooping and shooting arrows at anyone who stuck their head out. They even attacked the Vikings and the Moors, plundered monasteries and generally kicked the shit out of Europe, though it's not the done thing to be proud of that, and it's not my reason for mentioning it. Then they reached the Atlantic and realized that the prairie had run out. It was not possible to ride right round the globe, whooping it up, because there was an ocean to be crossed. There was nothing for it but to clamber up onto the stagecoach — over the wheels, unfortunately. The Carpathian Basin

was once a sea itself. Had we only arrived in time, we would have become a seafaring people, with our very own sea, not a historical one, not one so soaked in blood, not a rented weekend cottage.

In a matter of days Belgrade is turned into a modern city. Cameras record the demos from every conceivable angle. Wherever you go, it's all being recorded. People know they will be on television somewhere, on a German, Italian or English-language channel, and anyone with anything to say looks all round in search of a camera. The word was with the inkjet, the face became photo, the voice — magnetic tape, and there was evening and there was morning on the sixtieth day of the demonstrations.

A makeshift stage on Avenue of the Serb Princes. A celebrated diva harangues the audience about the victims of the past. Now a veritable Antigone, people speak in whispers about the fabulous breasts she had when she was still in films. We listen in profound silence, pressing a bit closer to one other, gazing wistfully at her bosoms as they ripple proud and free in the breeze of the eternal Yugoslav summer. The man's face is indistinct: it could be any one of us. He gently caresses her hips, they are drinking Montenegrin beer in the Bay of Kotor, then drive off to Dubrovnik and make love in the sunset.

I wake at daybreak. There is no dawn chorus. I sit up in the armchair and listen hard, but — nothing. It was an old Chinese trick, the birds couldn't roost because of the noise. I came across a half-frozen Balkan turtle-dove in Friendship Park. It was perched mutely on a branch, a suicidal tamagochi. On the map, Yugoslavia looked like a large squatting bird. Montenegro was the legs, Macedonia the tail, Serbia the wings, Croatia the neck, Bosnia-Herzegovina the lungs and stomach, Slovenia the head, Istria the beak. Perched on the shores of the Adriatic, it contemplated the boot of Italy.

Demonstrating with peanuts. You stand and chew, and in the meantime you're forced to use your head. You imagine you're not just demonstrating, you're also eating peanuts, distancing yourself from the event. Munching peanuts impedes any attempts to chant, clap or let anyone hand you anything. A pound of peanuts will keep you going in the cold, oil your insides. The real pros have peanuts, cigars, a hip flask and a silk scarf. They fill their pockets in the morning and get an early start, fingering the peanuts as if they were rosary beads. They shuck them in their mitts while on the march, murmuring monkey-nut mantras. They crunch non-stop throughout lengthy campaign speeches, standing up against police cordons, in traffic jams. When it gets boring they pick bits of peanut from between their teeth. Peanut husks are biodegradable, politically non-aligned. Demonstrating with peanuts amounts to a world view. They're also good for making friends. How about some peanuts? Masticating together as they demonstrate. He cracks a shell open for the girl then has her eating out of the palm of his hand.

Montenegro (Crna Gora) is a country with a delightful-sounding name — one vaguely recalls it is associated with bloody battles. History is the opium of Eastern Europe, it gets the adrenaline going. Montenegro is Serbia's seaboard, without which it would be landlocked within the Balkans. A guy from Montenegro at the student office.

He's not a nationalist, he doesn't mean to hurt anybody, but whenever he sees the Bay of Kotor he gets a lump in his throat. My pals and I didn't have to fight for Transylvania or the Polish-Hungarian border. I don't know if I would even defend Lake Balaton, if it ever came to that. I may be Hungarian, but whenever I see the Bay of Cattaro, my stomach starts to churn and I get a lump in my throat.

ma, mad, media, magyar, martyr, magnet, Macbeth, Mardi Gras, Mother Mary, mantra, mastermind, mafioso, macho, machine, magi, monkey-nut

Power to the pupil! The student posters have an air of the Commune in Hungary after the Great War. A handful of misguided youths, they say on television, but what a handful, says Dušan. He laughs at the right places. It's not his first time, you can tell. Packaged punch-lines at the press office. He's become strikingly professional in a matter of weeks. The official unit of measurement for the demonstrations is the handful: one handful=twenty thousand students.

They will only lose if they become craftier than their opponents.

Street theatre with police complicity. Macbeth in khaki shorts on a birdshit-splattered sidewalk. He's utterly mad, he's crowing like a cock in front of the police cordon at five degrees below freezing. Lady Macbeth is washing herself in her

nightdress. They roll round in the filth, with chewing gum and sunflower seeds sticking to their bodies — a heroic performance. The audience are heroes, too. Everyone is a bit of a hero, even I am touched. The circle of spectators slap their hands together against the cold — automatic applause. The cops are not moved, they stand rigid, like posts in a fence. Lord and Lady M. took leave of their senses in vain, the time is not yet nigh. Perhaps when the witches of Bosnia, Croatia and Serbia mingle their tongues in the same cauldron. When the plum-trees of Šumadija do come to high Belgrade hill.

In the nineteenth century, southern Slav language reformers chose the Herzegovinan dialect as the Serbo-Croatian literary language — an uncorrupted stage of linguistic development that had survived amidst the austere rocks of Herzegovina. But Tito had not even grown cold in his grave when the Virgin Mary appeared in Međugorje to speak to the faithful — and she spoke Croatian, no two ways about it. She introduced herself as the goddess of peace and called on people to pray for peace, which surprised the faithful as there was peace already. The mass graves in the area were gathering

dust. People had long forgotten that during the war women and children were thrown into the nearby ravines. The Virgin's message instilled in people's hearts a genuine desire for peace in that biblical landscape.

Mary, claimed the children who reported the vision, was a woman of about twenty-five, of medium height, and wore a blue dress. Every Thursday she'd send a short, horoscope-like message via a young girl (another Mary). One example: 'Today I beg you to make a special effort not to be led into temptation!' She chided the faithful if too few of them showed up, warned them of the approaching danger, and asked the assembled to pray with rosaries, which is considered kind of queer even in the Taizé community. A full penance consists of three Credos, eighteen Our Fathers, and one hundred and sixty Hail Marys. The basic unit was one tenth of that: one Our Father and ten Hail Marys — five minutes for an experienced believer. At that rate, one can work three times round the rosary in an hour and a half.

According to the chosen children, the Mother of God looked just like in the movies. After the premiere, the village was flooded with the faithful and so became a holy place of pilgrimage in the midst of the mountains (*međugorje*), with the visitors outnumbering the native residents. Had the Mother of God come a year earlier, Tito could have heard the good tidings, too. He knew Croatian from his father's side of the family, while his Slovene mother intended him for the priesthood. A mother has to understand, though, that you just can't butt into poker games when there's money on the table. It's unlikely God was ignorant of his mother's charitable deeds. He never made a secret of his sympathy for Cain, for instance. God intervenes, to the deep regret of the Serbo-Croatian language.

At his trial Gavrilo Princip declared himself to be Serbo-Croat.

Giovanni Capistrano longed to die a martyr's death. He took his role-models from the walls of

the local church: pictures of martyrs riddled with arrows, broken on the wheel, crucified, strangled, skinned alive, quartered. He daydreamed that one day he, too, would be painted on a wall, but reality is more cruel than the world of frescoes. Every day a new failure and a new penance, a further detour from heaven. He fought in the front lines, but on seeing his determined countenance even fanatical janissaries avoided going up against him. His father had been a mercenary in King Louis I of Hungary's Neapolitan campaign. Giovanni made a career for himself by persecuting the Jews. When things got hot, he took the advice of his superiors and turned against the Muslims. The Turkish siege was his big chance: if he survived that, he'd slip off the list of potential saints. As a Crusader leader, he unquestionably distinguished himself in the decisive battle to relieve Belgrade by charging the Turkish artillery against orders. Being still alive after the battle, he broke down in tears, feeling miserable and abandoned, but the Lord heard his prayers. His kidney problem flared up, and his haemorrhoids bled so profusely that he was unable to stand up to greet the king. He quietly bled to death on a bed of straw, just as he wished. The merits of his case were brought up in the Vatican, but Hungary was soon divided, and with that his chances of canonisation went down the drain. Two hundred and fifty years later, after the recapture of Belgrade, he finally manages to pass through the eye of the needle.

* W–G, p. 100.

I see an MDF flag, then Sándor Lezsák waving it as if he were in slow motion or cleaning a window without using Jif. He is clearly indulging his nostalgia, for a moment he is once again lionized by a unified crowd. He's standing on the podium next to Vuk Drašković. Even his hair is still streaming just a bit in the wind, and the flag with the tulip motif is being dipped to right and left by one of his trusties, a bodyguard or delegate. An awkward smile. Lezsák too is a former literary talent, but he has nothing to fear now. He is waving, arm and wrist equally slow, spurning the dust to win the prize: his hands are Teflon-coated. On behalf of his people and party, he salutes and supports the crowd as one, bringing a warm, symbolic embrace.

I get stopped on the way home. Allegedly I gave a speech along with Vuk. I am '*the* Hungarian', all rolled into one, and therefore a bit of Lezsák as it were. Seen in that light, we're on the same side, the Hungarian side. The Serbs return the gesture. They invite me to a party. Mileta and Danica are waiting at the door. No need to explain, they too heard my speech with Vuk.

'You and I are — we.'*

In the beginning was chaos, but we decoded it and understood everything, because we could read between the lines. Now we have to decode what we meant by the 'everything' that not so long ago seemed so clear-cut. In the Sixties Kádár emerged from the quelled revolutionary bubbling, and in the early Seventies our parents began to breed at an unprecedented rate. How can I explain to a teenager now that the better future we once sang about is here today, because the better future always comes. How can I explain that he will never understand? It's as though I were looking at my own parents, who believed that it would last for ever. Dear Mum and Dad, this is the country you wanted to emigrate to! You don't even need to learn another language! How can I explain that the change of régime in 1989–90 was the school-leaving exam, and that the old order passed away at the party afterwards? Our teenage rebellion swept Communism away, the new soft democracy crowded out the old soft dictatorship. The era that had treated us like children and held us back from growing up suddenly collapsed and vanished into thin air. And I stopped growing. My generation had supposed things would carry on as before, which they didn't, but we carried on pretending to be the way they

had always wanted us to be. A conspiratorial consensus of our parents over our heads, a mute orgasm with revolutionary momentum. Because of what happened in '56, Hungary didn't have a '56 in '89. Our parents had children instead, and brought them up to stay alive. And now we are going to live.

A guy on a bicycle weaves between the cordons, circling between the two lines. The cops have received no orders and don't budge. They pretend not to see him waving, hands off the handle bars, to the cheering crowd. When the traffic signal turns green the pedestrians run into the street and occupy the zebra crossing, when it turns red, the cops beat them back. Arrest the red man, the crowd chants. A policeman accidentally steps on my foot, and apologizes. A scene fit for a finale. Don't mention it, just a little Balkan parley. We saw it through together with the cops. Without us they wouldn't be around either. Nor would Eastern Europe. Without us, even the West wouldn't be to the west. Even its Coke has a

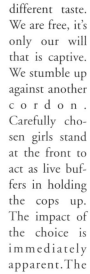

different taste. We are free, it's only our will that is captive. We stumble up against another c o r d o n. Carefully chosen girls stand at the front to act as live buffers in holding the cops up. The impact of the choice is immediately apparent. The way they puff their chests out for the foreign cameras is impressive. These are among the outstanding mom-ents of the Belgrade events. The cops are enjoying it, and so are the girls. Around us are red, amber and green traffic lights, glances caught in the flare of the flashbulbs.

n

nagyapa = grandfather
naptár = calendar
napszemüveg = sunglasses
Nagy Szerbia = Greater Serbia
nosztalgia = nostalgia
nevek = names
nem = no

When my grandfather was the age I am now, Gavrilo Princip shot the imperial heir-apparent. A fateful encounter of failed student and future emperor. A meeting which conferred immortality on both. And death. They did not know one other, maybe they exchanged a look. How do you do? Princip and the Prince, the prince and the pauper. One thing is certain, they both heard the shots. In the depths of parks ever since Gavrilo Princip statues shoot at Franz Ferdinand statues. Trench warfare between Gavrilo Princip Streets and Franz Ferdinand Avenues, a gun battle of memorial plaques, museums, medals, films. In Sarajevo, they pulled down the statue of the crown prince. The crowning achievement of his life was his death, which gave millions a cause to die for. The First World War began as a blood feud. When my grandfather was the age I am now, his fate crossed that of another. Both men were called up for the Imperial and Royal army. Both were sent to the Italian front and then, during the Russian offensive, both to Galicia. Both distinguished themselves. Josip Broz and his company captured an eighty-man Russian platoon, while my grandfather, during a surprise attack, picked up twenty-one shell fragments and several medals. When they wanted to amputate his leg, he pulled a gun on the surgeon and ordered him out of the operating room. Within one year both he and Josip Broz lost consciousness during

hand-to-hand combat, and both were taken prisoner. Both woke up in hospital, and both, still delirious from wound fever, were haunted by earlier traumas. My grandfather thought they wanted to cut his leg off, whereas Josip Broz accused the saint in the icon hanging above his bed of trying to steal his clothes. After several failed escape attempts, the revolution caught up with them in Russia. Josip Broz was seized by the Bolsheviks and enlisted in the International Brigade. While lying next to his Russian wife, he suddenly stumbled on the meaning of historical inevitability. I hate to think what might have happened had my grandfather ended up in the hands of the Bolsheviks. In the hospitals where their lives ended before the century came to an end, the century in which everything was stood on its head, Tito's leg was amputated and somebody stole my grandfather's clothes.

Sava Babić, head of the Hungarian Department at the University of Belgrade, offers me coffee. He's trying to worm out of me something about

Lajos. Is Zilahy a common name? But then he wouldn't dream of saying he's related to *that* Babits, though I know because that brainy chap László Márton, who knows everything, told me

so. All of Lajos's works have been translated into Serbo-Croat. He's the best-known Hungarian writer in the Balkans. Every serious bookshelf boasts a complete edition of Lajos, bound in leather. It's a common name. Svetislav Basara is introduced to me as the greatest living Serbian writer. He tells me about his childhood with Lajos. Between the two world wars he longed to be in Budapest, in the milieu of the *Fatal Spring, Two Prisoners* and *The Dukays*. Basara is a royalist. He went on the wagon after his wife bore him twins. He looks like a teenager with plans — plans involving a king.

nature, nation, nightmare, neighbour, no name, no sweat, note, NATO, naff, nanny, nectar, naked, novel, now or never, Nostradamus, nostalgia, Nosferatu, nose-job

The riot police, looming out of the fog, come marching down the embankment. The aesthetics are a bit too blatant, perhaps, but authentic for all that. Some people start to run but most stand transfixed, as if watching the filming of a costume drama. In this scene, medieval men in armour march in formation, the clatter of shields and thud of boots endowing the squad

with an air of heightened solemnity. Their movements are not robotic — loose-limbed more like, liberated, after having had to stand idly around for so long, and fired up by a will to fight. Neither overhasty nor sluggish, more with the leisurely gait of someone going out to check the mailbox, who knows full well that it won't run away and a steaming-hot breakfast is waiting for him. He's just popped out for a moment and happened to spot something in the grass, some large object, a forgotten ball or a pair of sunglasses, and he proceeds to kick it aside.

The Turks named it after the Hungarians, the Hungarians after the Bulgarians, while the Serbs, who fought on both sides, simply called it Beograd, the White Castle. Belgrade always lay on the border, shifting between north and south. It changed hands several times, just like most other European capitals. The Bulgarians took it away from the Avars, the Avars from the Byzantines, the Byzantines from the Goths, before which it was Roman, and before that, Celtic. The Celts wrote no history books.

'The opposite of no is yes.'*

Nándorfehérvár — the Bulgar White Castle as Hungarians used to call Belgrade — was Hungary's most important fortress during the waning of the Middle Ages. Three different sultans attempted to occupy it: the parallel ruins of AD 1440, 1456 and 1521 — or *anno Hegirae* 844, 860 and 925, depending on your point of view. The siege of AD 1456 is what the Hungarians refer to as the 'victory of Nándorfehérvár', which for the Turks was the year AH 860. It so happens that AD 860 was the year the Magyars first arrived in Pannonia, except back then they were called Turks by the Byzantines. The castle finally fell to the Turks on 29 August 1521. Five years later, to the day, came the battle of Mohács, and twenty years later, again on the same day, the Turks occupied

* W–G, p. 104.

Buda. It could be a national day of mourning, the Hungarian Kosovo, with as much justice as October 6th.*

There were portents of an imminent Doomsday: an apocalyptic heat wave across Europe, the appearance of Halley's Comet in the heavens. His Holiness had the brainwave of ordering that church bells be rung at noon each day to encourage the Crusaders. The papal bull and the relief troops were late in reaching Belgrade, which is why Hungarians to this day think the noon bells toll for them.** Serbs, on the other hand, think their tsars were eating with golden knives and forks when the princes at the other courts of Europe were still grunting around on all fours like pigs. Pope Calixtus III, for his part, considered the victory his own doing, and when he heard the news declared August 6th a Catholic holiday.

To this day, the Hunyadi express runs into Belgrade's main station at noon.

Sometimes, on a rainy February afternoon, you stand alone in the crowd. You are a stranger, surrounded by strangers. You walk around half-asleep in the drizzling rain. It will come to an end without being noticed. When no-one's interested any longer, the first demonstration-free day will pass without anybody knowing. Someone sneaks up behind you and whispers in your ear: this day and this protest will last for ever, and will begin again every day.

ny

nyakkendő = necktie
nyelv = tongue***
nyugat = west

---

*   On 6 October 1849, thirteen generals who had led the Hungarian army in the 1848–49 War of Independence were executed by the Austrians at Arad — the 'Martyrs of Arad'.
** According to the papal edict, church bells were actually supposed to be rung at 1 p.m.
*** 'Look up the entry for tongue. Be careful because there are two entries for tongue!' W–G, p. 72.

National Defence Day had ended too early. It was no use Gergő and me keeping our peckers up now. Uncle Al took us home in his own car. He had confiscated our Young Pioneer* neckerchiefs. No doubt I'd be prohibited from all patriotic duties from now on, never again allowed to recite Petőfi's *National Song* — 'On your feet now, Hungary calls you!' — or to defend my homeland, just because for once in my life I had the cheek to tie my neckerchief on a place it shouldn't be! Uncle Al is a verbal genius, able to speak in keywords and free-associate with adverbs, every utterance a language reform: language is his neckerchief. As for me, if they won't let me be a Pioneer, I'll be a writer, and what's more I'll write that down. With bitterness, but straight from the heart, I shall write nothing but the truth. Ex-Pioneer and goal ace, finalist in the nation-wide Russian competition, several times winner of Budapest Twelfth District's poetry recital competition, who could bring tears to the eyes of his music teacher and the girls' choir with his inspired rendition of 'On your feet now, Hungary calls you!' I wonder what would have happened if my voice had broken! I squandered the best years of my life on the Movement, with no defecting to Paris at the age of seven like Sophie Brünner. Instead of French mesdemoiselles, I have to listen to Uncle Al conjugating verbs after taking another one hundred

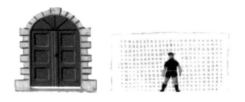

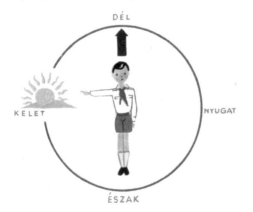

and eighty degree turn in his sentence, making the verb agree, at random, with the subject of three sentences back, reaching the hairpin bend with a rising inflection but tossing in a full stop without warning. Then he just looks, something symbolic, expecting us to understand. No sweat, how could we not understand! Sweat — not. It's not never going to end, we're going to rot away right here, in elementary school, and as the months roll by they will shrink us ever further with ingenious medical instruments. They look inside our little pants, and what do they see?

New Year, newsreel, neurosis, new age, nuclear

After losing the battle of Kosovo (Field of the Blackbirds) in 1389, the Serbs fled north and everything shifted a bit with them — blackbirds, field, Bulgarians and White Castle as well. Hungarian and Serbian have a lot of words in common but the meanings have changed. For example, our word for 'milk bread' means 'cake' to them, and our 'scone' is their 'pie'. But then the Hungarian word for 'hen' is what Serbs call a 'sparrow owl', and their 'hen' is a 'cockerel' to us, though it's a matter of perspective, of course, whether you think of that as our 'cockerel' being called 'hen' in Serbian, or their 'hen' being called 'cockerel' in Hungarian. The Yugoslav and Ugric words point to a common origin, and you can't ignore the fact that on old maps the southern border of Hungary once stretched several hundred miles further south. From here it is but a short step to clasping the southern Ugrians to our bosoms. One can only hope the Finns don't start splitting hairs over it. A brotherly federation

---

* Pioneers and Little Drummers were compulsory Communist youth organizations for different age groups. Little Drummers wore blue ties, while Pioneers, over ten, had red ties.

would come in handy, and not just to blow hot air as with the southern Slavs, but in a more profound, semantic sense — one in which there would not be eternal shedding of Central Yuropean blood but instead the sea would lick our united arses. Then we'd get to the World Cup final again, for sure, and all we'd need is a catchy name: Yugars United, perhaps. We could even stretch it to bring in the Kurds (a little Turkish yoke). The Vietnamese too, for that matter.

Seržan brags that he has never studied any languages and yet he's trilingual. Since the war, Serbian, Croatian and Bosnian have become three languages. They divided it up amongst themselves, like Bosnia. Each insists on its mother tongue. The Bosnians are looking for their roots under the Turkish occupation, the Croats prefer to pay for interpreters. There's no communicating in a tripartite language, it's inconceivable for a Serb to speak Croatian to a Bosnian. But then what language will the child of a mixed marriage speak if both parents insist on using their mother tongue? *

A politician is delivering a speech. He says that quality is a function of the trust placed in it. Time is a causal relationship, a matter of fabricating the future from the present with the help of the past, he says. That is his job: the future, past and present, but most especially the future. That's his forte.

'The world is everything that is the case, taken together. Anyone who is born comes into the world.'**

I was born in the twenty-fifth year after our liberation. Lenin would have been a hundred years old had he still been alive, and St. Stephen one thousand. A sort of personified nil point between the two of them, like the zero kilometre marker at the Chain Bridge in Budapest — that's my starting point.

1970: the year Boeing's 747 jumbo jet was put into service, Soviet-American disarmament talks began, the first stretch of the Budapest metro was opened, Brazil became World Cup champions for the third time, and Hungarians were allowed to travel to the West every three years, so there was something to lay money aside for (Junior Savings Account). My parents enrolled me in elementary school when the one hundred thousandth Ikarus bus came off the production lines. The Skála Metro department store, opposite the Western Rail Terminal, went up in parallel with my progress at school — one floor higher each year, with a choice that was 'all but flawless on all floors'. It was finished when I reached eighth grade. Travel was in the air. My mother had dipped me in the Black Sea when I was still no more than a foetus. Maybe that's why I've suffered from a salt deficiency ever since. I wake up at night, and Mum is dog paddling in the dark. Somebody is shouting from the other shore: Glass of water coming up! My parents sacrificed their careers as engineers to help quench my thirst. Mum became a maths teacher, Dad trafficked people: he sold geniuses to the West. He travelled in software, covering the world. I wouldn't have

---

* 'When I put food in my mouth, I sense its taste on my tongue. I can tell whether it is sweet, salty, sour or bitter. The tongue is a sensory organ. When I speak, I wag my tongue.' W–G, p. 107.
** W–G, p. 154.

minded being a plaything of the Great Powers myself once every three years — for hard currency, of course.

We hardly noticed Austria, but we were shit scared by the time we were approaching Munich. There it was! We shivered in the summer sun. The West appeared cold and merciless, my brother and I needled one another. We wanted to go home and were glad we weren't part of this. We really were scared. We even saw American marines. They were pumped up and had tattoos and roared around on Yamaha 500s without going anywhere. They stared at our red Lada like at a snail shell after rain.

Despite our entreaties, Dad would not turn back and didn't stop till we reached Cologne Cathedral. He would take us to a McDonald's at the cathedral, he promised. The young, the Jews and the Commies, they're ruining the world! shouted an unshaven joker, a homeless *Gastarbeiter*. He practically knocked me down as he staggered across the square, bottle in hand. That was the first time I had seen a tramp and a Gothic cathedral. I stood for hours in front of the two towers, I didn't even care about McDonald's, my parents couldn't drag me away. I decided to travel the world, and visit the Cologne cathedral of every country I went to.

According to Johannes Lichtenberger's *Prognostications*, the book of prophecy he wrote in 1488, Cologne cathedral would be the setting for Armageddon, the final battle between Good and Evil in which the Lamb tussles with the Beast. The struggle between Christian and pagan forces would end at the golden apple tree of Cologne. Gáspár Heltai, the mid-sixteenth-century Transylvanian preacher, printer and Bible translator, worked this prophecy into

his chronicle of the Magyars, and through him it was picked up by the Turk Ibrahim Peçevi. Peçevi expressed the hope that the Padishah would reach Cologne. Cologne harbours the tombs of the three Magi who visited Jesus in the manger. During the Second World War ninety per cent of the city was bombed flat. The cathedral remained intact only because the Allies used it as a reference point when on their air raids. The finger of God, so to say.

O

olvas = read
orosz = Russian
orvos = doctor
ostrom = siege
osztálykirándulás = school trip
Osztrák-Magyar = Austro-Hungarian

The Albania Palace is Belgrade's *fons et origo*, its point of reference — the dead centre where the imaginary zero kilometre post stands from which the spokes of the city's avenues radiate and its house numbers begin. It is also the place where the demos begin every day and where the cordon of riot cops is set up — a live and kicking nullity of several thousand fuzz at the capital's zero point.

My Russian teacher says I will never understand Slavic culture until I have read *War and Peace* in

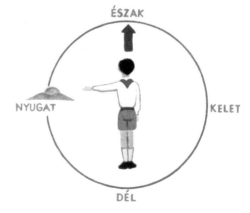

the original. She read it while riding the Trans-Siberian Express, there and back. I'd rather read *Crime and Punishment*, as that would let me off at Moscow. Maybe it would be enough just to work through the crime part, then for the return leg I could fly Aeroflot (such a splendid word that — like cologne made from recycled poison gas). Language was part of the pretence. We pretended we knew Russian. *Noo!* Forty-five minutes every day I listened in Russian, nodded in Russian, sighed in Russian, even set out *War and Peace* next to me on the bench.

It never entered my head that knowing another language could be useful. Knowledge was a prerequisite for growth, something to be acquired for its own sake. If you wanted to grow, you had to do your homework. Russian was something we learned because it's a splendid language as well, of course — not that Hungarian isn't fantabulous, mind you. Back then, only Russian teachers spoke Russian, and they were all women of about fifty with dyed hair, a militant ethnic minority with their own tribal rites. They had a particular obsession for roll calls. Taking a head count before every mission was a matter of life and death. The only Russian soldiers I saw were in war films, and even they were dubbed into Hungarian. The first time I saw them in the flesh was when they withdrew from Hungary. The Cold War had come to an end, and so did peace. Since there was no longer any sense dying for it, the Russians were selling off their equipment for token sums. My pal wanted to buy a parachute and I acted as his interpreter.

Parashoot yest'ye? — Is there a parachute? I asked, but I began laughing and dropped the *ye* at the end. Good lord! The Russian for 'is' and Yankee 'yes' sound the same! Maybe it had been worth studying after all. 'Yankee go home' or '*pashli damoi*' it comes to the same thing. The occupation is just a line on the map, an accent, a conjunction. Not the tanks, not the eight grades, not Misha the bear, but a signature on my report card. The lance-jack answered in Hungarian: two bottles of vodka, he said, raising two fingers, because there were two of them. He asked how I

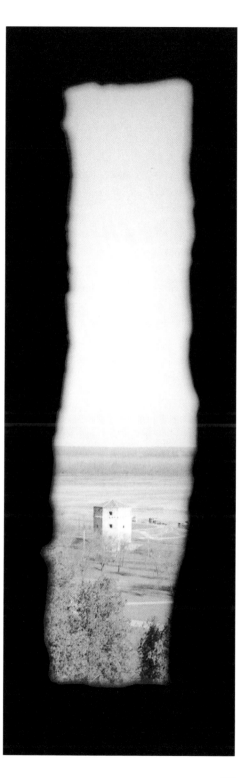

was doing in school. I resented his familiarity and grumbled *noo-noo*, just like I had seen in *And Quiet Flows the Don*. He said he had a son, too, Sergei, and he knew it was not easy for us either. What would we say to a Kalashnikov? Or how about this pistol? It's like letting Cookie Monster loose in a sweet shop. A good job I'm not sweet-toothed. He'd throw in a cartridge clip as a gift, let's have a drink to the good old days. The good old days when

I wasn't yet alive and our fathers were merrily killing each other off — I should drink to that with an enemy soldier who is speaking to me in my own language! *Ege segedre,* said the NCO, his *nazdarovye* sticking out a mile. *Egészségedre* 'to your health' or *ege segedre* 'to your ass' — close enough. Sergei was also called Sergei, like his son, but we could call him Seryozha. He handed me the bottle and quoted Petőfi impeccably. Hungary is poetry, he says. I tell him that a group of Hungarian scientists had identified what they claimed were the remains of Sándor Petőfi in a grave in Barguzin but it turned out to be a woman's skeleton. He wasn't surprised, he said, Russia's a big country. He wasn't in the least pushy — helpful rather. He didn't particularly want to go home, he said. He'd got used to being in Hungary and liked Hungarians, especially the women, winking at me as though he expected me to know what he was talking about. I gave him a Pavlovian wink back, because I knew that's what you do when you talk about women. We didn't want to bother him any longer, but he begged us to stay, still speaking Hungarian, of

course. I'd better watch out! Could it be he didn't even speak Russian — an Ob-Ugrian double agent, perhaps? We back away, waving. When we reach the door, he calls after us: How about a few hand grenades into the bargain?

'What would happen if every child went to school when he or she felt like it? If one day he or she turned up for class at seven o'clock in the morning, the next day at nine o'clock, and the third day in the evening?'* Classes have been suspended at Belgrade University. Foreign correspondents are sleeping in the lecture rooms. In the evenings there are voluntary study circles and film showings. The dean gives the students an ultimatum: they will all be rusticated unless they stop running around the streets and go back to their desks. The next day the college students of Belgrade move their desks out on the street. We learn for life, not school, as Seneca declared.

Oliver brings bars of chocolate for his brother, Teddy, who is standing in the cordon. He studied karate and as a riot cop is making three times as much as Mama, who is a school teacher and cries her eyes out thinking her two sons will end up fighting each other. What times we live in! (If only I'd had the chance with my own brother!)

* W–G, p. 128.

Teddy graduated from the Sports Academy, he is a teacher of martial arts. Oliver is a medical student, he wants to cure people and save the world. The whole family shows up at the cordon to take pictures. Teddy is roaring with laughter, Pa is blowing his whistle for all he's worth, Mama is crying, Oliver is wincing. The journalists love it. Teddy calls home: there's going to be a rumble. Oliver asks in fun if Teddy would beat him, too, if they were to meet by chance during a clash. Sure, that's my job, his brother says. On the day set for the rumble, Oliver pelts the cordon with stones and hopes his brother is on the receiving end. Oliver is studying to be a brain surgeon and holds an impromptu anatomy class in front of the fuzz. With the help of a skeleton, he explains the occupational health hazards of being a policeman. This is a skeleton. Let's put a flak jacket on it. See, the spine runs down the middle and is deformed if too big a weight is put on it. He points to various small bones, explaining their function and what happens when they fracture. On the subject of risk factors in the workplace he sets special emphasis on potted plants falling from window sills. He discusses the skull in detail. When that's hit the brain can be damaged. But that's not such a bad thing, he says, because at least then you know you have one. The cops start grumbling. This is not their idea of law and order.

'Stone is hard, clay is soft. Bone is hard, flesh is soft. We eat soft-boiled eggs with a spoon and slice hard-boiled eggs.'*

Oliver showed how tear gas affects bowel function as well as the eyes. Specifically, when your brain is about to explode, your eyes feel like they are spilling out, your lungs constrict, and you realize you've been poisoned, you panic and break into a run. You only stop when you see people running towards you. By then it's too late, however. Your brain has been restored to its proper place, your eyes did not spill out, and your lungs have reflated, but then you realize you've filled your pants.

A trial judge lays down the law to the policemen in the cordon, genning them up as to how long their sentences could be, given that what they are doing is against the law. Article so and so of the penal code says . . . , and then he reads the pertinent paragraphs. He offers impartial advice, telling them what lines of defence can be cited, if it comes to that. The police chief signals to his men to take the provocateur away. They start towards him, but the lawyer whips out his ID card and holds it up, just like in an American film. The cops pull up short. Their chief screams: Get rid of the guy, now! They snap to it again, but now seven or eight more judges appear, all with their

* W–G, p. 78.

ID cards, and shout out contrary orders — they should arrest their superior officer, for instance. The cops stand confused before the line of IDs, feet rooted to the spot. They're afraid to take another step, the respective spheres of authority are far from clear. Cursing, they back off and rejoin the line.

If only everyone had an ID like that!

The letter O is a perfect circle found in the middle of the Hungarian alphabet, every point of it being equidistant from its centre. Accordingly, the centre of the letter O may be regarded as the centre of the Hungarian language.

The Austro-Hungarian Monarchy. It's good to live in a big country, it beats living in a bunch of small ones. Watching the changing countryside from a train, speaking several languages, making a mixed marriage, vacationing by the sea, screwing the ethnic minorities, oppressing the Other in oneself, going down to the pub, being relative, confessing, forgiving, waking up with the taste of freedom on our lips.*

ominous, obvious, October, occult, occupy, Ottoman, optical, optimist, origin, officer, orange-blossom, oxymoron

Zdenka is a bluestocking who specializes in demonstrations. As soon as she sees a stranger, she thinks she's in the West and crosses her legs. She goes to the officer in a miniskirt that is so skimpy, they won't even let her do the photo-copying. She goes out for a quick little demo and comes back five minutes later with three Italians in tow. She's told to dress properly, she's distracting attention from the demonstration. Wide-eyed, she asks why? Didn't she just bring them some Italians?

The crowd, who have the sober outward appearances of groupies for a punk-folk band, demands as one that the opposition be made to account for their actions. You can't look into the same mouth twice. No need to make the rounds of it — the whole country is here. There are even some people from the other side of the border. Men in sheepskin caps drink home-made hooch from hip flasks and the healthy spirit of protest goes to their heads. Buses have been arriving since early morning, each with a picture of Milošević by the driver's seat. They wave like idiots, thinking everyone's been waiting for them, the relief troops. Zombie protesters with a faint whiff of resurrection. They want Peace and

---

* 'Any country which is not our homeland we call a foreign country.' W–G, p. 87.

Freedom, Slobo and Mira. A blend of amnesty and amnesia in various octanes. The equipment is handed out. Everyone is given a flag or picture plus a packed lunch with an apple. The last forty years parade down the street, socialist faces in period costume. Gold teeth and iron teeth in the same mouth. A class outing in search of fashions past. You could bet on the geographical region just from the jacket styles. This was how old men and women used to dress when I was a kid. I wonder if, twenty years ago, they deliberately wore clobber that was twenty years old even then in a deliberate show of setting themselves apart, or were they already wearing the same clothes as today? The pro-government forces sport leather coats and raincoats in autumnal shades, the opposition wear quilted jackets with a definite preference for gaudy colours. Still, there is some overlap. Here are all those who fell for the idea of Yugoslavian brotherhood, believed Tito would last for ever, and now believe Milošević is a saviour, and our ancestors were driven out of Paradise over an apple. Who bought the assertion that the Great October Revolution was actually in November, that everything was the fault of the Americans, and the streets of Belgrade were prey to a handful of hooligans. Everybody who fell for everything is here and accounted for. Everybody who bought a line, took the hook, guzzled and lapped it up, swallowed it whole, gobbled it up, gulped it down and still refuses to believe that they've been had, that they're cannon fodder, spooks from a crypt, suckers . . . Yugoslavs.

The charge by the Kirghiz cavalry swept the Croat infantry away. On Easter Day, Josip Broz, sergeant in the Royal and Imperial army, a lance lodged in his back, was taken prisoner on the outskirts of Okno, which means 'window', in what was then Austrian Galicia. He regained consciousness in a monastery that had been converted into a field hospital. The nurse tied a red ribbon to his bed — a sign for the dying.

ó

óra = class
óriáskerék = Ferris wheel
ólomkatonák = tin soldiers

The last history class that I recollect from high school was about the First World War. András Porogi gave a lively description of the changing political and military landscape. Sarajevo, Masaryk, Marshall Foch, Bosnia and Bessarabia were condensed into one hour — all words containing syllables that connote shitting or screwing in Hungarian. The dissolution of the Monarchy was thus a physical experience for all of us. Porogi managed to keep a straight face. I then understood something about history.

oasis, ode, OAP, oracle, obey, omen, over, overjoyed, open town, oh my!

People took fright, ran out onto the street, and saw what they feared coming towards them. But by then it was no longer frightening. I'm going downtown on what was once Tito Boulevard with the riot police coming up behind me. If I stop, they will still keep on marching. Nothing is said, but everyone knows the rules: force and counter-force. The crowd is piling up in front of the cordon. As soon as we outnumber them we'll turn round.

'I'll go if you come, too. If you won't come, I won't go either. If man were able to fly, Pete would fly over the sea.'*

The third full moon of the demonstrations. It rose early. An albino peacock is screeching in the zoo at the foot of the castle. It gives me the creeps. Has the cracking of ice-floes on the river frightened it? Or is that just how albino peacocks screech? Eerie, even its voice is colourless. Palaces have always put freaks on display. They have albino tigers at the gates to Caesars Palace in Las Vegas. I'd rather be an albino tiger in Vegas than an albino peacock in Belgrade, if there was a choice. There isn't. A Ferris wheel is spinning emptily, a virtual big wheel — whatever you look at carries a deeper meaning to pull you in. You're sitting on a gold mine. All you have to do is dig down to the Celto-Romano-Gotho-Graeco-Avaro-Bulgaro-Hungaro-Serbo-Croato-Turco-Germano-Austro-Russian bones, the bones of mercenaries, stooges and allies of every European and Asiatic nation, the Swedish, Tartar, French, Swiss, Mameluke, Syrian and Persian warriors who are buried under this strategically important hill. On a clear day you can see all the way to Byzantium.

* W–G, p. 61.

71

The albino peacock screeches, sizing me up with its beady eyes. A lost soul.

Ö

összever = beat up
ördög = devil
örökkévalóság = eternity

In my dream two guys beat me up so badly I couldn't get out of bed the next day. I had to stay between the sheets and carry on dreaming the dream. Intimidatingly, they turned up every day to inquire about my well-being. My well-being, don't make me laugh! They scribbled stuff into my hospital case-notes, but I couldn't read it because I couldn't get up. They left a phone number where I could reach them at any time in my dream. Then they didn't show up for a long time. Nothing happened for weeks. I couldn't take it any more, I called them up. It's me, I said, what do you want? Oh, it's you, one of them said, you again. What do you mean again? I asked, this is the first time I've called. Sure, sure, they all say that. Before long you'll be denying that this is your dream. They tried to shake me off and wished me sweet dreams, but I wouldn't take no for an answer, I demanded an explanation. The taller of the two leaned close and whispered: Do you really want to know? He looked me in the eye with his blank gaze, and then I realized: Good Lord, I'm talking on the phone! How could anybody look me in the eye? By then, however, they'd put the phone down. The line has been busy ever since. Though maybe I didn't call them, after all.

official, opinion, occasion, observer, obituary, Olympics

In the Seventies, a band called 'No Stone Unturned' had a big hit with a song that went 'If there's an eternity, and it has a name, then Tito is that name.'

ő

ősember = caveman
őserdő = rainforest
őrségváltás = changing of the guard
ősz = autumn

'In far-off countries where it is never winter there are huge rainforests. It is dangerous to go into a rainforest.'* Rainforests are also called jungles (see more about them on p. 13).

At two o'clock in the morning, the crowd begins a countdown in unison. Every hour is like the end of the year. When we reach zero, a girl wraps herself round my neck — a blonde or a redhead, I can't tell in the amber lighting, but no matter, she's already wrapped around someone else's neck. For the benefit of the browned-off cops, students read out of basic electrical-engineering manuals and Kant's *Critique of Pure Reason*. When it is time for the changing of the guard,

the band plays 'When the Saints Go Marchin' In', and the spectators applaud the departing detachment. The cops try to march out of step to the music but that only produces a weird synchrony of its own: go-go boys, armed to the hilt, in military S&M gear. The new boys don't bat an eyelid and wiggle their hips a little mechanically. You can never practice enough. Clockwork toy soldiers march off towards the cordon. One bumps into a boot and carries on marching on the spot; another breaks through under the shields and, to stifled whoops from connoisseurs, sets off across the cleared stretch of no-man's land for the far side of the square. The police chief doesn't notice, and they march side by side, little robot and big robot, bobbing cosily along on their Duracell batteries.

'We humans were not always the way we are now. A hundred thousand years ago, man was still a caveman.'** On the other hand, cavemen were not always like us.

p

páva = peacock
papírrepülő = paper airplane
politika = politics
piros = red
pillangó = butterfly
pietà = pietà

'The colour red looks like this: Blood is red. Poppies are red and so are ripe cherries. In

---

* W–G, pp. 113 & 153.
** W–G, p. 113. No caveman was like another — unless they were identical twins. Even then one can't know for sure.

Hungarian there are two words for red. In the calendar holidays are printed in red. Scarlet red is a little bit lighter than crimson red. Look up crimson on p. 110.'*

Politika is being given a public funeral. Thousands stand in silent mourning, a farewell from

the near and dear to a long-ailing friend. *Politika* is dead, and it's not in the papers. Candles are lit for its soul. *Politika* was a daily newspaper. Now it's in bad shape, its windows have been smashed in, there are red paint and rotten eggs on its walls. *Politika* was once *the* daily paper in Yugoslavia, even Tito did not mess with it. But those days are gone. Flowers are strewn in front of the entrance. A couple of thousand ex-readers at the bier of the non-aligned world. On a winter's evening, by flickering candlelight, people grieve for *Politika*.

Halfway across I got leg cramps. I waved to the life boat to go on when a butterfly alighted on my hand. At the time I was under the influence of my cousin from Nyíregyháza who'd read all of Tandori's works. I caught flies in our apartment and then set them free from the window, several times a day at that. We were both tired and confused. The butterfly perched on my forehead, but we figured that just as I would be unable to pull it down it would be unable to lift me up.

* W–G, p. 118.

So there we were, drifting between the northern and southern shore of Lake Balaton. A swallowtail with curly antennae and a pretty intelligent face for an insect. It couldn't fly off because its wings were soaked through. When I took a closer look, I could see it was a butterfly genius: it had such a perceptive look, and it was looking at me. Its defencelessness gave me strength. With even strokes, I set off back to where I'd come from, as if I didn't care whether it was the northern or the southern shore, Acapulco or Aden, as if I didn't care what the halfway was the half of. I thought back through my past life about all the butterflies I had maimed, ripped apart, stuck with pins, left out in the sun in jam jars, trampled underfoot, slammed with a tennis racquet, sprayed with insecticide, dissected with a razor blade. But abandoning this butterfly in the middle of Lake Balaton somehow seemed inhuman. I'm swimming with arms only. My face is getting sunburnt, my ass is freezing, I hate myself. And I hate big words, but it's big words that keep me going. The coach says I've got talent, but even I can't talk under water. Under water, fat chance! I'm afraid it will fly away and tumble into the water again, and then the whole thing will have been in vain. But I'm also hoping it'll fly away and free me of the need for explanations. I'm swimming on my back, keeping my head out of the water. The butterfly is probing my nose with its antennae, feeling the hairs in my nostrils. Halfway through the cross-Balaton marathon

I had developed leg cramps. I floated on the water and tried to relax. Above me, in the sky, a cloud-shaped giraffe swam past. It stretched out its neck for cloud-shaped leaves, but they were scattered by the wind. The giraffe's neck turned into a noose through which it slipped its head and vanished from the sky. Does it have such a long neck in order to reach the buds on tall trees, or have the trees grown so tall in order to escape the giraffes, or both at once, with a compromise being reached? A cloud, in itself, is a compromise, a frozen lake in the sky. To watch a cloud from beginning to end, watch it fall into Lake Balaton.*

party, party member, partisan, paper plane, patriarch, parasite, peacock, police, politics, pi, provocate, prole, parole, profit, prophecy, privy, pill, pillow, pilgrim, panic, picnic, Pioneer Park

G. called. Today is the ten thousandth day of my life, he had worked out. I could write a diary about just one day, he said. Ten thousand days, that's seven leap years. You can't always get what you want. I checked it for myself: the ten thousandth was yesterday. Late again! I dedicated the ten thousandth day of my life to the letter P.

Three thousand cops in front of the Albania Palace, across from the *Yugoslovenska knjiga* sign. One fellow is shoved through the shop window. He shatters the glass and becomes entangled in a banner advertising Philips: 'Let's make things better.'

In the afternoon, a co-ordinated aerial attack on the Supreme Court: Belgraders bombard their public buildings with paper airplanes. Bombing as catharsis is part of the city's psyche. Everyone has a bombing story. Belgrade's immortal soul is reborn in the craters with which its endlessly lustful enemies continue to impregnate it. Belgrade bereft of its bombs would be like Paris without the Eiffel Tower, New York without the Statue of Liberty, Budapest without its bridges.

*   See the entry on clouds on p. 40.

Therapy and performance art. If outside help doesn't come, Belgraders will do the bombing themselves. A human being runs towards a wall at full tilt, arms flapping: he might take off at any moment.

Milorad Pavić entertains with literary sleights of hand: a Tarot novel, a menu-card play, and his *Dictionary of the Khazars*. Pipe in hand, grey-moustached, a supercilious smirk — a Serb Sherlock Holmes. Six months ago he still supported the war and Milošević, but last night he spoke at the student protest. He signs a book for me. The words are intelligible, but I can't decipher a single letter of the writing. What do you make of that, my dear Watson?

I am invited to attend a conference on Serbian nationalism in Belgrade. During a recess I hear that in Kosovo the cops are shooting at Albanians from helicopters. The speakers agree that Serb nationalism is more extreme than the Hungarian variety, the Serbs have not had a big kick in the backside yet. In a dream I saw

Mother Teresa and Sylvester Stallone, both of Albanian descent, with Sly gently supporting the fragile angel. Mother Teresa spoke to me in Albanian but I understood what she was saying. She asked me not to jump to hasty conclusions. If I find the right voice, I will be understood. Sylvester nodded, adding that Bengalis are the best poets. He raised an index finger to the lips of his camouflage-caked face. His angel had fallen asleep, and he tiptoed out of my dream. For days I was haunted by their compassion. Why can't they be on CNN together? They could have their own show.

q

From the stormy centuries of the Aztecs. It had been prophesied that their banished god would return on the far western fringe of the Habsburg empire: he would have light skin and a beard, even the year tallied. Cortés appeared at the right moment, the year of Venus. They took him for a winged serpent. He, for his part,

grabbed their gold, laid waste to their capital, and had their king, Montezuma, put to death. While the Spaniards were busy taking Tenochtitlán, the Turks captured Belgrade at the third try and blew up the bastion from which Dugovics had flung himself to his death, carrying with him the Ottoman standard-bearer and thereby stopping him planting it there at the

second attempt.* After that the Kingdom of Hungary fell apart and St. Stephen's crown ended up in Vienna, along with Montezuma's feather head-dress. The Hungarians eventually got their crown back, but Aztecs still protest in front of the Kunsthistorisches Museum, saying it's not an art work but a relic. The museum claims the Aztecs themselves filched the feathers in the first place from a neighbouring people they had subjugated. A plumed serpent, indeed, whatever next! Quetzalcoatl, that's all those filthy Indians need! They probably only heard about him at summer school, anyway.

quiet, quest, question, quality, qwerty, quarantine, quo vadis?, quote, quake, quack, quitter, quintessential, Quetzalcoatl

Q is the twenty-ninth letter of the Hungarian alphabet. There is not one word of Hungarian origin with a Q in it. Gavrilo Princip is Belgrade's

red-light street. Possibly Gavrilo himself frequented it before turning his back on his studies and leaving for Sarajevo. A small token of sympathy, like the audience vote on a TV talent show or a statue that isn't spattered with pigeon shit. Maybe heroes of independence attract the girls. Unfulfilled dreams. There is dire need for a post-monarchic, urbanistic analysis of the relationship between prostitution and anti-Habsburg sentiment.

r

rádió = radio
reklám = advertisement
rendkívüli állapot = state of emergency
Rigómező = Field of the Blackbirds
rossz = bad

Besnik Restelica, one of sixty-six Albanians arrested at the end of January, died in his cell at the age of thirty. According to the official news report, BR tied two short-sleeved T-shirts together and hanged himself on his bunk bed. The Kosovo Liberation Army called for armed uprising against the Serbian occupiers.

I'm travelling on the train with a Hungarian girl from Novi Sad. Nice, very nice. Like stepping into a front room in muddy boots. The train halts, but I don't get off. Ruins by the Danube, with the walls leaning over at even sharper angles than the hillsides. The ruins were designed to

*   See the entry on Dugovics on p. 11–12.

look as though they are about to topple, but not quite, unlike the houses under construction opposite, which only looks as though they were standing, but not quite, even after ten years. A Godforsaken station, suspended between being, leaving and standing still. A different

state of mind: to East European eyes — order, to Buddhist eyes — death. But anyone who alights needs to feel that they've arrived. That's why station buildings are so reliable. The train stops and at any moment you might find yourself arriving in a town where you once lived. The girl waves. A picture-postcard smile wreathes my face. Historical experience, everything is transient. On crossing the threshold, kindly wipe your feet. So go on, wave! I'm waving too, as you can see. None of this would have happened if it hadn't been for the Austro-Hungarian Monarchy. I am a guest, and you're the colonial ware.

On Republic Square a group of lost pro-government supporters join the anti-government demo by mistake. The speaker is lauding Serbia: how it could be fair and free, free and fair. The old codgers nod: Well said! As they nod they turn round and look at all the young people: How nice! Then one of them notices a picture of Vuk Drašković in his neighbour's hand and jumps back as if he'd stepped on a turd. What's this? he shouts. Treason! The crowd turns and sees thirty copies of Milošević. Dumbfounded silence. The Kosovars snatch quick looks to right and left, the Milošević pictures exchange glances. Now what? They're standing in the wrong place, sorry. They don't want to attract attention and would get going, but they are surrounded by the crowd, which is not in a good mood. Milošević is taken away from them, their caps are knocked off and

filled with eggs and vegetables. Scared shitless, the old fogies start running the gauntlet in an unfamiliar city, with boiling water being poured on them from upstairs windows. Street fights break out in Belgrade. In front of the French Embassy, sobbing old folk are cowering in parked buses, with students all around, leaping up and down with poles that have been stripped of their placards. Belgrade's new coat-of-arms: a young protester rampant throwing eggs at an elderly peasant gardant wielding an apple at the window of a long-distance bus. In the city centre the cops intervene to defend the contras. The crowd flings eggs, potatoes and rotten fruit over the heads of the riot police at the anti-demonstrators, who throw placards back. The local forces are bolstered by fresh ammunition in the form of several sacks of potatoes. Volleyball over the cordon. One of the contras parries a cabbage head with a Milošević poster, batting it back into the opposition's court. Net shots slither down the police visors. The apples have nearly gone, the contras throw everything back. The price of eggs and tomatoes is on the rise since they can only be used once. The state-building drones wriggle awkwardly in their body armour and helmets.

'Crying is bad, laughing is good. Being afraid is bad, being happy is good. The opposite of bad is good.'*

Two visors clash. The two riot cops grin, they had forgotten their heads are bigger in helmets. One lifts his visor, and we light up a Gitane. We

* W–G, p. 122; you can read about good on p. 68.

get pally, though he does ask me not to take a photo of him with the opposition paper, and he slips *Democracy* into his upturned groin pad. He warns me about the stocky guy who is slapping his rubber stick in the palm of his hand. I was warned the very first day that the city was not safe — it's full of cops. The riot police have had special barracks built for them. Belgraders count riot cops instead of sheep to get off to sleep.

Diverse fashion trends are on display on the catwalk. The basic three-piece of shield–rubber stick–revolver is part of every uniform, but a flak jacket and gas mask accessory bestow the air of an élite detachment. Seemingly minor but important variations of detail: truncheons of varous lengths, helmets with or without plexiglas, pushed up, pulled down or even, in a few instances, perched cheekily on the forehead. For the riot cop a sexy chin is a definite plus, because when he's in full gear it's the only part that shows. Other accessories include machine guns, grenade launchers — very macho — and, increasingly in evidence, walkie-talkies. The new line of longer body armour looks like a khaki-coloured house coat. The flap of the groin pad, when pinned up, comes in handy for stowing all sorts of equipment, lending its wearer a leisurely, devil-may-care attitude, and can even serve as a muff for ice-cold hands. An officer relieved of truncheon and walkie-talkie can hook his thumbs on the upper, sleeveless part of his vest, as with a pair of braces, in a cocky, foppish pose worthy of a yuppie police squad whose fast-improving financial prospects will soon overtake those of the bourgeoisie. As fashion dictators, these public-servants-cum-mannequins have joined society's progressive strata. No longer grim guards, they seem to be strolling even as they stand.

radio, radical, ruin, ritual, régime, regret, romance, riot police, rotten spuds, rush, Russian, red, revolution, random

The Serbs have a word sounding like '*retch*' which means 'word', while the same sound is

part of a word meaning 'crackle' in Hungarian, as with a radio. Milošević's wife is Mirjana Marković. They have a daughter called Maria. Maria has a radio station. They own the media. Retch, retch, retch.

B92 has been banned. The radio station was shut down by a power failure just when they were in the middle of comparing Milošević's rise to power with Hitler's. Oversensitivity or pure coincidence? The Great Powers will not put up with this, people say. And indeed, Western stations let them use their frequencies. They carry on where they left off on Voice of America, Radio Free Europe and Deutsche Welle. The independent papers likened it to the Second World War, when the country was under occupation, people listened to the BBC — and, of course, there was Hitler. Analogy-fixated: they might look for a less remote war. The next day the protesters stop in front of the Radio building and cheer the free press. A window opens and a DJ leans out, mike in hand, to broadcast the news live. But he does not say, you are the news, feel free to interrupt, thank you very much. He misses his cue and does not say: do whatever you feel. Now that *would* be news.

A history major warms her backside, wiggling it in front of a bonfire in the street, then turns her back on the cordon and repeats the action. Somebody gave me an apple. That's what I'm chewing right now. History tells us that bonfires burn out, songs lose their meaning, and girls in jeans grow old. We stand around like idiots, no longer knowing why we are chasing them, and even they forget why they lead us on. Only the fire remains the same. Our Magyar ancestors, so it is said, once went out to hunt a stag but bumped into some women and settled down instead. Where would they have ended up if they had continued the chase? The Belgrade correspondents are bored to death. God! says the *Der Spiegel* reporter in the Hotel Moscow café, another day of demos. Nothing's actually happening — no mass shootings, no Party secretaries jumping off balconies. Ashes eddy up to the tenth floor, along with the bleating of sheep stamping round the fire, which is burning like a shepherds' campfire, an urban pastorale flickering in the shop windows. In the pedestrian precinct a symbolic flock: matronly ewes, manipulated opposition sheep, coalition lambs who can be talked into anything. They're here because this is very Balkan, and it can't go on like this any

more. The flock from Zlatibor are demanding democracy, free elections, a solid system of law and order, freedom of the press. They've had enough. The penny has dropped even for the dumbest blonde, runs one Belgrade graffito. Sheep don't talk a lot, they have strong presence. They are no quitters. Their eyes are on the sides of their heads. They are chinless, and from

the front it looks as if they're constantly grinning. The sheep stop in front of the cordon and fix the gas-masked riot cops with their sheep eyes.

S

sapka = cap
síp = whistle
sír = cry
smárol = smooch
staféta = relay baton

It's snowing again. Spring is late. The university's dean is away on a skiing holiday. Every day thirty thousand students demonstrate to call for his dismissal. He kicks off down the hillside, and thirty thousand people pray he will miss a turn. Oh, to ski through one's life, slalom through protesters, drink mulled wine and then glide home, straight as an arrow, between two police lines. I would like to live in a country where the ski instructors go on demos.

One has to own a whistle. Mine is made of tin with a cherry-stone for the pip — loud enough to split your ear drums. It hurts at first, but then it sets you going, pulling you out of passive contemplation. In order not to lose your hearing, you have to shrill louder than anyone else.

Irritation, properly channelled, becomes a source of pleasure, and if that doesn't work, you can always buy yourself a pair of earplugs. You have to develop your own rhythm. By vibrating your vocal cords, you can even produce animal sounds. Whistles fill the spaces between demonstrators, leaving no room for doubt. Equally, they are instruments eminently suited for self-expression, you can blow them any way you choose. In addition to the financial crisis and factory closures, one should also call attention to the sudden boom in the whistle industry. Demonstrators can take their pick from mass-produced, die-injected plastic models to hand-made, one-off wonders. Besides a whistle, it's worth buying your child a balloon as well. Like a buoy, it shows his position should he go adrift in the crowd.

A balloon tied to your child can avoid your having to drag him along behind you for hours on end, you wouldn't hear a cry for help anyway.

Let's not talk, let's whistle, says a friend. As long as we whistle no-one can tell we're all thinking something different.

Along comes Vuk, tugging heart strings as he goes. On his way to the demonstration, he says, he met a little old lady who was crying. He asked her why she was crying. Why are you crying, granny? Vuk Drašković asked the old biddy. She said she was crying because she had had a dream about freedom. In my dream, the little old lady said, there were no more cordons, and I could come and go freely, as I please. That is what the old biddy said tearfully, and now Vuk shares this with us, parading the invisible old dame, waving her above the crowd.

Last night I dreamt of being a super-hero in a Yugoslav metropolis. With my special double-lens glasses, I saw through the cordons and the double-dealing politicians. I was lonely, as super-heroes tend to be, and trailing dejectedly homewards when Vuk Drašković came up and asked me why I was crying. You tell me, Vuk. Why am I crying?

Couples kiss during the protest, aroused by the crowd. They osculate with their eyes closed, carried along by the tide. One girl peeks with one eye: is the city still there? They're being swept towards me, whistle in my mouth, peanuts in my hand, it's too late to get out of their way. At the last moment they crash into a column. The couples give the crowd renewed energy. They kiss the kissers, making love not war in Serbia. Protesting with smooch-proof lipstick, meeting the love of your life on a demo — an East European story with a Hollywood script.* I held her hand while Drašković was speaking, put my arm around her shoulder when Djindić was on, and gently pulled her to me when Vesna Pešić appeared. Let's just leave it at that!

sabotage, sacrifice, ski trainer, scandal, scarlet, scapegoat, scenic, slivovitz, savings, safe sex, smack, smash, smooch, spark, sugar, soul kiss, go for sushi

Because it was needed for his biography, it was decided that Tito had been born on May 25th. Being a simple peasant boy from Zagorje, Tito knew only the month he had been born in, not the date. It was actually May 7th, but by then the

* 'If you head eastwards, the west will be behind you.' W–G, p. 109.

25th had been designated Youth Day and a nation-wide relay marathon was held in his honour, so it was too late to change. People were impressed by Tito's youthful energy. He is claimed to have had lovers even when he was in his seventies. He revived a Habsburg custom by offering to stand as godfather for the ninth child born to any family. Youth Day was broadcast on TV throughout Yugoslavia, and the relay baton was handed on as if it were the Olympic flame. Every city had its youth representatives running with its own, home-made relay baton. I saw one of the finishes from a recording: a young girl runs into a crowded stadium, sprints along the red carpet and gives Methuselah a kiss. This was already getting a bit embarrassing during the Seventies. There was even a competition for the most artistic relay baton. Later on the constituent federal republics of Yugoslavia each took turns to run the event, which continued even after Tito's death. The last relay baton was made by the Slovenes: it weighed thirty kilos and was carved from marble. They made a poster to go with it, which was inspired by a Hitler Youth poster. The resulting scandal put an end to the relay.

While they are doing their small pre-demo chores, bored riot cops listen to a newspaper vendor's analysis of the political situation. One cop with an obsession for cleanliness is meticulously wiping his visor. Seducing the cops is a constant theme. Take one home and introduce him to your parents. The male student demonstrators are less enthusiastic about that. Instead, they bombard the cordon with condoms in a play on words that sounds good in Serbian but can't be translated. At least the cops carry rubbers.

The fashion craze provoked by the uniforms finds its ultimate expression in headgear. Dunce's caps, nightcaps, deerstalkers, fur caps, astrakhans, bowlers, top hats, sou'westers, bobble caps, skiing caps, pork-pie hats, jockey caps, derbies, flat caps, baseball caps, boaters, sailor's caps, miner's tin hats, eggshell hats made by art students, my Russian-looking *ushanka*, Stetsons,

birettas, general's peaked caps. Facing them, three or four thousand identical blue helmets.

SZ

számok = numbers
szabadság = freedom
szótár = dictionary
szappanopera = soap opera
szupernagyi = Supergran
szépség verseny = beauty contest

Olga, an eighty-six-year-old English interpreter who for years won first prize for the best-kept balcony in Belgrade, has become a symbol of the revolution. The crowd stops under her window, shouting Supergran! Supergran! Olga flourishes a banner, blows kisses and waves. When we pass below she is crying, her tears dropping on us. She wipes her eyes on the tricolour and tosses flowers on our heads. Olga, the best-kept balcony in Belgrade.

Serbian joke. Q: Who was the greatest Serb? A: Pasha Mehmed Sokolović, victor at Szigetvár and Tripoli. A Balkan success story, he was born in the Bosnian village of Sokol and at the age of eighteen was paid in to Istanbul under the 'blood tax' system. He learned Turkish and was

converted to the true faith. His exceptional ability as an organizer was quickly noted, and once he had established himself he sent for his family to join him. By 1546 he was commander of the Mediterranean fleet and took Tripoli. In the years that followed he popped up at various trouble spots of the Ottoman empire — Lepanto, the Don, Eger, the Yemen. It was he who built the bridge over the Drina. While beglerbeg for the Balkans, by then known as Mehmed-pasha Sokollu, he witnessed the massacre of the defenders of Temesvár. At Szigetvár he was the victorious grand vizier who kept the death of Sultan Süleyman a secret. During the siege itself the Hungarian commander, Miklós Zrínyi — as he tried to break out of the fort against heavy odds — was hacked to pieces. Several delegations of Hungarian envoys petitioned Sokollu for the return of Zrínyi's remains before he eventually acceded to the request, albeit reluctantly and only in parts.

In elementary school they taught us to write the letters of the alphabet next to one another. The words were in a book, like solutions; all you had to do was read. The dictionary had all the words that could be said. That was part of the world of adults, but I sensed that it was, in

some strange way, beyond them. Dictionaries had a superhuman authority. Whatever you said, if it wasn't in one of those books, it had no meaning. Only when it was written down.

A dictionary juxtaposes words that you never find together in real life. It is a meeting-place

which raises the accidental to the status of law, like the names in a class register. A class register is a dictionary, too, one in which they keep a record of me, with my name, date and place of birth, my father's name and occupation. They know that my parents are electrical engineers, and I am the son of electrical engineers, which means that I probably know something about electricity. There were no writers in the class, that would have really put the thing to the test.

The alphabet seemed an unchangeable fixture, like lining up by order of height in PE class. At any rate, it stood outside time as we perceive it. Whose turn will it be today? I was already a word when I was born.

Every word in the dictionary is indispensable. Each one on its own is of no use, only together do they make any sense, like a class register. It's the solidarity of words that creates language, like the solidarity in a classroom. It could be anybody's turn next, and every day begins with a roll call. Our names are called out to see if we're still there, from A to Z, Almási to Zilahy, every single one.

stir, stern, stellar, stare, stairwell, stalker, stagger, stereo, storm, startle, stark-naked, steak, satiate, saturate, Saturday night, satellite, Satan, satire, star, starve, start, state-of-the-art, stakhanovite

Freedom is everyone's concern. It is not an empty word. It comes and goes freely, is free as a bird, its head reels from the taste of freedom.

Freedom is a state of being. Freedom is a feeling, a greeting, a hill in Buda, a newspaper. Freedom is freedom of thought, universal freedom, freedom of the press, freedom of the seas, a car — oh no, sorry, Pobeda's a victory. Freedom is a radio station. Free days, running free in the open air, let your thoughts run free! Free association, free-thinking, free verse, free-living, freewheeling, freeloading, free entry. Freedom in Russian, freedom in sign language, physical freedom, freelancing, freestyle wrestling or swimming. Freedom is a free kick, a free ticket, a free transfer, free love, kisses are free. Freedom is a free lunch, free time, a free house, let's go to Freeport. Freedom is a free phone, free spaces, free fall. The harbinger of freedom, the taste of freedom, the sweet bird of freedom. Freedom becomes her, his freedom is cramped, the limits of freedom, he hasn't got a free moment. Is this table free? Is this Freedom Square yet? One can be given a free hand, savour a whiff of freedom, not know what to do with one's freedom, devote one's free time to something, want to be free of someone. Freedom can be discarded, sold, exchanged, devolved, violated, curtailed, blighted, trampled underfoot, and a little bit of

freedom wouldn't hurt. Freedom is the Freedom Statue on Budapest's Gellért Hill, the land of the free, loss of freedom. Freedom is inalienable and belongs to us all, one freedom, two freedoms, people's freedoms. It is free agents, free trade, free enterprise, breaking free, feeling free, being free to roam. Freedom is freeing a city, freeing one's slaves, freeing oneself of one's calories. How free is freedom? Are we free to touch it? To smother it? To stroke it? To eat it? To have a small glassful? Freedom is there on the label: tax-free, fat-free, duty-free, sugar-free, alcohol-free, carefree. Free your mind! Freedom is a freebie for short, when the road is free and you're free to do it, time for a free-for-all, leave your body free, defend yourself freely, free yourself of your clothes, of your emotions, give them free rein, my soul soars free of its prison walls, come, freedom, bear me away on your wings! Freedom is a free bed, a free university, freemasonry. The bloody banners of freedom. Hang free, grow freely, be freestanding, have a free choice, feel free to walk around. What is freedom? Am I free to ask? Free sex, free range, thrust freedom upon or deny it someone, free oneself from an embrace, be freed of a sweet burden, be free to decide. Are you free for a dance, for a moment, for a bit of free enterprise? Personal freedom, free will. Freedom is freebooting, freedom fights. One can make free, be free-spoken, lose one's freedom. Give me liberty, and deliver me from the devil . . . Free me, oh free me, Slobodan Milošević.

Fancy calling your child Freedom, of all names. Wee Freedom, the love-child. There he is: Slobo photographed with his podgy little fingers and toothless grin. Freedom in its infancy.

Over here, Freebie! The big boys grab him and snatch his ice-cream cone. It is said that Milošević is suicidal by nature. If he falls, he's going to drag an awful lot of people down with him. Sloboda or Slobodan? — wizardry with words or irony?

College graffito* after a Milošević speech: Why say you love me when you only have sex on your mind?

'One thousand and one is more than one thousand. 1,001 is more than 1,000.'**

---

* 'A sign always substitutes for something: a sentence, a word, a sound. A letter, for example, substitutes for a sound.' W–G, p. 74.
** W–G, p. 143.

One night they run a beauty contest at the cordon. Everyone involved automatically becomes a contestant. Thanks to the women's votes, the Mr. Policeman prize goes to a riot cop with a moustache. Miss Student Protester is a short blonde. Attempts to get the winners to warm to each other end in failure.

It's the seventy-sixth day of protests by the local calendar. A scoreboard is used to keep track. Belgrade is in her third month. Everybody considers the child to be their own and wants to maintain the pregnancy, despite the pressures to end it. The mother's legs may be swollen, and she may feel nauseous at times, but when she wakes up, she looks great.

In the beginning was the Soviet avant-garde: they hoped to keep the revolution going by staging street performances. If art and life are one, revolution is the greatest theatre there is. You have to get your audience involved, convince them that their fate is in their own hands. They wanted to create a theatre that would make the man in the street think he was making history. They organized the siege of the Winter Palace, with thirty thousand extras. Malevich and Chagall gave a hand with the scenery. Chess games were played in the open air with real horses and hussars, real artillery and gunners. The passers-by had real guns. The civil war was on, and the White Army was approaching. Mayakovsky summoned his fellow-poets in verse, calling upon them to march in the streets. You're only a Communist if the bridges are burning behind you, Mayakovsky said in a poem entitled 'Order to the Army of Art'.

On St. Sava's day, a huge procession heads off for the unfinished basilica. It will be the biggest Orthodox church in the world once it is finished. The students parade with the gilded three-handed Madonna and a copy of a copy of the oldest Serbian icon, sent by the monks of Hilandar. St. Sava is the students' patron saint. God is on our side, Čeda shouts. The students pray for the end of winter and for the New Serbian Spring to arrive. The patriarch blesses the student protesters. Orthodox priests march shoulder to shoulder in black robes with thick beards and heavy crosses. As they pass, 'Highway to Hell' by AC/DC starts up from the loudspeakers. God's honest truth! I swear I'm not making this up.

t

talán = perhaps
tojások = eggs
tömeg = crowd
történelem = history
tüntetés = demonstration
tornaóra = PE class

The radio is calling on listeners with the names Slobodan Milošević and Mira Marković to kindly come to the cordon. There are several pages of Miloševićs in the telephone book. Everyone's got at least one acquaintance called Slobodan Milošević, it's just that nobody has a telephone book. Slobodan means Free — from the Turks, that is: it's a nineteenth-century coinage. A telling name, isn't it? 'Slobodan, they call you freedom / You're loved by one and all' — a Kosovar Serbian fraternal ditty available on cassette and CD. The namesakes soon gather, form into pairs and go up to the cops to tell them it's all right, they can go home now. B92 says a base is being built on Mars and the Communists will be sent in ahead. It's an experimental base, they need die-hard Party cadres.

The contest between Spring and Winter, a time-honoured custom re-enacted at carnival. A staged drama of the siege of Belgrade offers a précis of all the earlier sieges. The whole of Belgrade serves as a stage. The city is divided into two teams, like in a carnival competition.

Winter's task is to preserve the old values and defend the rights of the lord of the castle, whereas Spring aims to introduce new rules into the general confusion and infiltrate its men into the castle. Winter's costume is a dreary bluish-grey uniform — an allegory of death. There are no women in Winter's team. The assailants are dressed in motley, individualistic garb — they're Spring, after all, the embodiments of change. The choreography consists of orchestrating head-on clashes, big solo pieces, and a corps de ballet of thousands. The static element is lurking death, symbolized by a row of helmeted skulls. Winter's soldiers don body armour. They are archetypes, like the tortoise and the crocodile, hard-carapaced primordial creatures guarding the Prince of Winter. Prancing groups of merry pro-

testers, grins on their greasepainted faces, bait the armed guards. For the duration of the festival, this joust of the masks and the helmets draws onlookers and foreign visitors into the action, bringing the city's traffic to a halt. Everyone is free to choose sides, but there's no ducking out of the contest. Winter's movements are clumsy but purposeful, menacing in the unrelenting regularity of their steps. The essence of the movements of Spring's host is an unpredictable, capricious cavalcade, in consequence of which their number is impossible to estimate. The dynamics require that the attackers be in the majority. They're the ones demanding change, wanting to batter down the old walls, making a hell of a racket, blowing whistles, beating drums, tooting trumpets, shrieking, huffing and puffing, grumbling — anything to scare the defenders, who, due to their static stance, are in no position to respond.

'Every living creature grows. It starts life small and gradually gets bigger. A baby is barely 50 cm in length, whereas some grown-ups are taller than 1 m 70 cm.'*

Life does not come to a standstill in Belgrade. People go about their business in the midst of the demonstrations. Some join the demos according to a regular timetable, others put in a spell on their way to work, or when they need to walk the dog, or read the papers during the speeches, or come down for a quick drink with friends. The demonstrations have become part of the fabric of the city's life.

Marching on the spot in PE class: that's how we'd advance if things ever turned serious. For the time being, though, we're Little Drummers, junior Pioneers, rumbling up hill and down dale like a powerful locomotive, just as our song says, carrying the germ of goodness inside us, like the protein in a pimple — nasty little man-eating proto-Pioneers. We do as we are told in PE class. We're constantly growing, in a growing competition, and we're made to stand in line, with me at the end.

* W–G, p. 42.

In nursery school I was at the head of the line, but my growth was uneven, my teachers said I lacked discipline. I have the calm of a nursery-school Lofty and the aggressiveness of an elementary-school Titch. My report book looks as if it had the measles: the spattering of red would make an albino proud. My Pioneer neckerchief is blue, like my eyes. I carry a germ of goodness inside me, a Little Drummer without a drum. My deskmate, who used to be shorter than me, got to be first in the line-up. You can't tell when we're sitting, but it's awfully embarrassing when the class has to jump up to attention. I kneel on the desk or lean over to tie my shoe-laces, pretend I am about to do something. I *am* about to do something.

The giraffe is the tallest animal. When it sticks out its tongue, it can reach six metres. It sleeps standing up, gives birth standing up, and is born standing up. Its Latin name, *Camelopardalis*, indicates a cross between the spotted great cat and the ship of the desert — a Freudian slip in some kind of Icelandic kenning. As an offshoot of European rationalism, the cameleopard is comparable to a mole cricket or a bullfrog. A giraffe in good form can dispatch its enemies with ease, even kick a lion aside. The males use their head like a mace to fight for the females and, disgusting though this sounds, use their sixteen-inch tongue like a lasso to gobble up the leaves of locust-trees. The giraffe is a peace-loving vegetarian and in captivity lives to a ripe old age. It is distantly related to the camel, so it may still have things easier than a rich man going through the eye of a needle.

One placard under which I used to pass every morning I later saw as a badge, an extract of an extract from the Talmud: 'If not you, who? If not now, when?' The beginning of the fragment goes: 'All of us, if just once, will reach those who need us.'

On the eve of war in the Balkans, the correspondent for *The Kiev Thought* is travelling from Budapest to Belgrade. Because of the Serbian mobilisation, he's forced to disembark at Zemun and do the rest of the journey by steamship down the Danube. As he approaches the Serbian side, he is alarmed by the sight of old peasants in folk costume, standing guard with guns over their shoulders, and he recalls a Hungarian colonel on the train, picking his nails for hours on end, the miniature bars of Milka chocolates on snow-white tables, toothpicks wrapped in rice paper. The next day, in the café of the Hotel Moscow, he is touched by the sight of peasants marching off to war in their leather moccasins and sheepskin caps with fresh green sprigs pinned to them. The end, it seems, is inevitable, Trotsky once wrote.

Belgraders cheerfully part with the past, which is why I am here. It's not that the past could part with them. I'm optimistic, even if this happens every spring, because this feast is not about one winter but many, and there will never be another winter like this, nor a spring for that matter. And perhaps I shall never be this optimistic again.

In a dream I was in Yugoslavia, the snow crunching under my boots. An equestrian statue was getting drenched on the square, and a bearded man was giving a speech in some Serbo-Croat language. Yugoslavs were protest-

ing without a care in the world, pinning flowers in policemen's buttonholes. A girl in a jester's cap approached me with a steaming cup of tea.

Stop or I'll shoot! I say jokingly, pointing my gloved index finger. The girl stops short and, nearly tripping over in her confusion, scalds herself. The boys and I laugh. I watch

her bite her lip, rubbing the stain I caused on her jacket. My temples are itching, as though they were being scratched from the inside. I raise my visor and I twig.

I'm a riot cop. I have my orders to go to the pedestrian precinct and harass troublemakers. Violence is not my cup of tea, but if stones are thrown at me the blood goes to my head. We march in step, as we've been practising for weeks, a stiff-legged riot-cop corps de ballet. The crowd disperses steadily, without regard for age and gender. I'm no sadist, I take no pleasure in watching a woman get beaten. I don't beat her out of pleasure, but I can't be partial. I'm a link in the chain. One riot cop alone is no riot cop. I watch the faces pushed up against my plexiglas, insects on the night road.

While beating someone I have the unpleasant sensation that my rubber truncheon is shorter than usual. I measure it against the others. It seems small, shrivelled. I slip it back inside my body armour, I don't want to start a riot.

The walkie-talkie says action, and we stiffen into posture. Mine is the shortest rubber truncheon I've ever seen. In my dream I was a riot cop and my rubber truncheon was drooping. By the time I'd finished striking there was nothing left in my hand. The protesters were laughing at me. A guy in a Russian-looking hat appears and grins. I take him for a foreigner: nobody in Belgrade would wear a thing like that. I knock the *ushanka* off his head, the motherfucker, for smiling when my rubber truncheon is shrinking.

In my dream somebody sticks a cigarette tab in my hand. I raise my visor, and I twig: it's me in the *ushanka*, grinning from ear to ear. My heart skips a beat. Just when I should be setting an example. I start yelling at me. What the fuck am I doing among the protesters when I'm about to order an attack and these animals are about to smash my head to a pulp? If I want to get myself beaten up, I should go and find another square. I ask for a drag but it's too late, the radio squawks, I see myself blowing my whistle, and we march forwards. I am chasing myself and running away from me. The crowd presses tighter and tighter. I think of my fear and I strike, a flailing beetle, upended on its back. I am never the first to lash out, I leave that to the others. After that it's all the same, they'll hate my guts anyway. This way is at least honest. Yes, I'm a riot cop for the money. What did you think? Why else would I wear a gas mask? I think of my fear. I don't dare not to hit out. Screw you all, you fucking Gypsy rabble!

A writhing animal with a hundred arms and legs. I don't like blood. There's no need for blood here. Why hit him over the head when he'll fall down anyway? I can't see the *ushanka*, I hope I haven't hit myself. Anyone might have a gun. Why don't they shoot instead of all this jumping and jeering? What am I toting this sodding flak jacket for, then?

In my dream I suddenly come face to face with myself. My arm is in full swing and it's too late to stop it. The moment I strike my baton disappears. I wake up. I am me, but I can still see myself in the *ushanka*, running away with two plain-clothes cops on my tail.

I race back along Tito Boulevard and up Partisan Brigades' Avenue, just across from the protesters. I go the opposite way around the cir-cuit to the direction I've been taking every day. I try to give them the slip in the alleys behind Terazije. The Cyrillic letters are fading away, this isn't Belgrade any more. Rounding a corner, I am in Wenceslas Square, Prague. A hundred thou-sand people are shaking bunches of keys in the glimmer of cigarette lighters. We shake them together. I run out of matches and ask the pro-tester next to me for a light. One of the agents spots me in the flickering flame. They chase me through the Old Town, up into Hradčany Castle. Thousands of students hand in hand, a crowd winding along like a snake, with me crawling among their shoes and agents snapping at my heels. Through a beer cellar I reach Berlin. At the Brandenburg Gate I squeeze through a fresh gap, but I can't shake them off. They're coming after me past the Wall. Gumming a false beard to my chin, I try to blend into the dancing crowd, but you can't hide in a dream. They catch

up and converge on me in the Alexanderplatz. I slip into a side street and come out by the eternal flame on Batthyány Square in Budapest.

It is March 15th, the anniversary of the '48 revolution, and the rubber truncheons are busy. I try to reach Bem Square across the Chain Bridge but motorcycle cops are barring the way. The last thing I see is three men beating up a woman who's trying to keep her hat on with one hand. I want to help her, but the agents pin my arms from both sides. I fling myself into a ground-floor apartment, a shower of bloody goose-feathers drifts down from a duvet. I am in Timişoara, and the Securitate have surrounded the Lutheran parsonage. The congregation form a shield around Pastor László Tőkés. I dress up as an Orthodox priest, but the plain-clothes men still pick me out. I flee to Austria in a stolen Trabant, then in a Greek truck back to Tirana, but they can read my thoughts and arrange a riot for my arrival. Every street leads to yet another city, and in every city protesters are marching towards me — Sofia, Warsaw, Leipzig, Bucharest, Vilnius, Bratislava, Tallinn. In the Gdansk shipyard workers shake their fists as we run past. My dream has turned black-and-white: Prague at dusk, with tanks approaching — our tanks. Don't shoot, I'm Hungarian! The plain-clothes men grab me, yank me into a doorway and start methodically working on my kidneys. The dream steels my muscles, I fight myself free of the circle and head for home. The guards have vanished from the border. It is now 1956, and I am walking against the stream of the convoy that is heading for Vienna. Disguised as a Red Cross worker, I manage to get round the anti-tank devices on Széna Square. Through a shattered window I spot my men: the same trench coats, the same pitiless smiles. I won't give up now. I go down Light Street to reach Moscow Square. The only way is back, one last, never-ending thrust underground, towards Moscow itself. The city is under siege. I dodge from house to house, eliminating enemy snipers. A wall collapses on me and they dig me out in

Stalingrad. The Russians raise a barricade of frozen soldiers; our troops are at war.

Amid the ruins I arrive at a bombed-out square with a statue of Lenin meditating on the Great Red October in an oriental pose. He glances at me and his arms start spinning in the air at lightning speed, a hundred-armed Shiva with a cap in every hand. Lenin, a whirlwind in the maelstrom of history, blinks like a strobe light above the ruined landscape. The road leads through concentration camps, interrogation rooms and mountains of corpses, with the agents breathing down my neck. Shots ring out.

There's no stopping me now. A somersault and I turn up on Budapest's Andrássy Avenue in 1919. Horthy rides in with Son of White Horse, Árpád and the Magnificent Seven Magyar chiefs. They gallop through the city and flush out the

Red Peril. The 'Internationale' is played backwards: 'Rebmuls ruoy morfs rekrowey esira!' A spectre is haunting Europe. I shake it off and go out to the Trotting Course to enjoy the White Terror. I strut my stuff for the bad girls. I ensconce myself in the New York Coffee-house to sip a caffè latte. Across from me, two guys are peeking surreptitiously from behind newspapers. It's them, but I act as if I haven't noticed. I sneak out through the toilet window and escape across the yard, but they're waiting for me outside. In the crossfire I lose my hat, a paternal inheritance (my father has not yet been born but I'm already squandering it!). I fling myself into the past. A wide boulevard, Cyrillic letters, Oriental pomp, the snow crunching under my boots. An agent dropping on me from a balcony fails to surprise me. I expect them by now, proof that I'm not fleeing irrationally, that there is a point to my flight. The sleuths are on my trail. With my last reserves of strength I gain two weeks on them: they haven't switched to the Gregorian calendar yet. The flagstones are slippery, I lose my balance and slide on elbows and knees into a snowy square. I try to protect my head but nobody's beating me. Whining, they retreat as if their owners were calling. My pursuers stand puzzled on the corner of Nevsky Prospect. I'm standing in front of the Winter Palace. It's night-time and the square is flooded with light. The windows are heavily barred, but the gate is open. This is not how I imagined it, and besides I've been here before. I hurry along white corridors. The Winter Palace is an oversized hospital with no patients. The wards are whitewashed as if the vast, snow-white Russian winter were snowing indoors. An insurmountable rebuff. Whispering and hissing are audible behind a door, but when I tear it open nobody is there. I've been to the Hermitage before, but I'm lost without the signs. White shutters on the window. What happened to the chandeliers? I've needed a pee ever since Belgrade — normal protester anxiety. I go back to the entrance and relieve myself in the gateway, as if I had just run in from the demo to warm up for a moment. Face to the wall, my eyes closed and mouth agape, I raise my head to the sky. A moment of grace. I grow numb. Now, just once more. I open my eyes and see that it is not a wall, not even a rubbish tip, but a giant riot policeman's boots, down which my steaming piss is rolling on both sides.

The guard was standing in front of me. I recognized his fur-lined coat, his hooked nose and his long black Tartar beard. He was enormous. He bent down and asked if I wanted to enter, pointing to the door. I fell to my knees and prayed fear would overcome my curiosity.

In my dream I was in Belgrade, standing in the middle of a winding puddle in a gateway. Surging crowds on the street. As I button my fly, I spot the two guys standing in the gateway. I understand that I can't flee any more, because every crooked path I take will lead straight to him, and to wake up now would be just as much cheating as not being born. I am the beginning and the end, the protester and the riot cop, the revolution and history, the giver and the taker, the Master and Margarita. I am my parents' greatest blunder, and I'm the only one who can make good their mistake, I'm the unwanted love child.

I walked back to the square as dawn broke. The treacherous still of silent films sat heavily on the flagstones. There was a muffled crump from the guns of the 'Aurora'.

When the riot cops knock me down for the third time I start speaking in the plural. We speak in the plural as we did in the Seventies, but now we've really got it together. We dance together, we run together, we are knocked down together, we might even be comrades.*

'Instead of possibly we can also say perhaps.'**

In secondary school it transpired that history was written after the event, which was a bit of a bummer at the time. Our sense of security was shaken. The past could change at any moment, and all we can do was watch helplessly. We are spinning along with the Earth at this crazy speed and time is out of joint. It was no good people saying that history had to be written, and that was a time-consuming process, or the past was constantly changing and history was getting better and better, so one just had to be patient. Rome wasn't built in a day either! Those reassurances didn't help at all. I wasn't convinced. By our second year the past was changing so fast the printer couldn't keep pace

*   'The word mi is used for asking questions.' W–G, p. 101. Note, however, that the Hungarian word 'mi' means 'what' or 'we', depending on context.
** W–G, p. 39.

and we might as well have chucked our old books away. All we knew about history is that it hadn't happened like that, and it was working for us. There would be something to talk about if it caught up. Only they didn't tell us how we would recognize it. How would we know when it was the real thing? Would it come knocking on the window one day? Oh, it's you! Come on in! Good to see you, History, old chap. How are you? Spill the beans . . . If indeed there is such a thing. Maybe it has to be made up. How many people did that take? Is whatever happens to lots of people history, whereas what happens to one person isn't? Imre Nagy, for instance, was hanged. Is that history or a private affair? And if Imre Nagy's hanging happened to all of us, then did my Imre Nagy and your Imre Nagy sit down at the same table, or are they two different individuals, maybe not even one, and then is that my private business or your public concern? Is it only history when something happens, or is everything I remember history? And did what happened to me happen to others too? And if something happened to others, why didn't it happen to me? Do we have a common past? Are there any Magyars at all? Did they exist in older times, or was it only in older times that they really existed? And if the Magyars settled in the Carpathian Basin one thousand years ago, then who are we? And who will be Magyar one thousand years from now? Will they have bows and arrows, saddles and horses and marry the elder brother's wife if she is widowed? Throw Molotov cocktails at Russian tanks? Hide in the cellar? Wear a fascist armband? Will your typical Magyar have a tent, a fiddle and a refrigerator? How many wives or husbands or children will he/she/they have? Will they have orgasms, period pains, difficult days? Will there be any women at all? Or only women? What colour eyes, hair and skin will they have? What will be the average Magyar chest size? And for that matter, what language will they speak? Once upon a time there was a great plain, and on this plain lived the Magyars, then one fine day they jumped to their feet, pulled the arrows from their arses, and galloped off into the sunset. They were never heard of again.

100

timetable, tease, telephone, tap, tobacconist's, treat, trademark, thrill, target, tears, Talmud, tale, Trotsky, traitor, Tito, tiptoe, Tudjman, turkey, to be continued

The Belgrade events have revolutionized the concept of sealing off space. Cordons permit both internal and external spaces to be segregated in the best possible taste. A police cordon brings an ambience to the streets, which, when supplemented by water cannons, contributes immensely to an environmentally friendly, self-cleansing residential ecosystem.

CNN has been covering the demos in Belgrade for the last three months. Never before has a soap opera been so cheap: betrayal, violence, love and national aspiration — all in the daily life of a city. Giggling teenage girls, crowd scenes, amateur cameo roles. Milošević and his men miscalculated when they pulled it off the air. People took to the streets out of sheer curiosity. The new graffito: I think therefore I turn off. In Belgrade everyone has an equal chance of making it onto the screen. The news is broadcast live, with everyone on a separate channel. The day the protests ended, the art students hung twenty-yard rolls of canvas over the dean's office windows from the roof. Written on them, in black letters, were the English words: To be continued.

ty

tyúk = hen

In her diary Mirjana Marković, wife and right hand of the dictator, writes that she likes to read the novels of Shakespeare and Chekhov at night. That woman has no weak points, an enemy of hers once said.

'The hen is a bird. A domestic animal. A fowl. It is very bad at flying.'* Hens lay eggs, the symbol of this revolution.

* W–G, p. 146.

u

utód = heir
utca = street
ugat = howl

The Germans and the British took turns to carpet-bomb Belgrade during the Second World War. Post-war Yugoslavia became a hotbed of Cold War fever. In 1953 Tito still had tanks trained on Trieste. When the Yugoslav airforce shot down two US planes on the Austrian border, the New York papers called for a nuclear attack on Belgrade. You can hear the hit from Kusturica's *Underground* fifty times a day. It's dark, it says. War overshadows everything, it says. The sun shines no more, nor does the moon, it says. You are not, nor am I — then suddenly there's bright light, a flash in the sky, and nobody knows what's shining.

A warning sign in the corridor of a prefab apartment block: Danger! Fire, smog, earthquakes, bombs. It briefly describes what to do if anything happens. The warning signal for a nuclear attack is a twenty-second siren, repeated twice more at fifteen-second intervals. 'In the event of an unexpected nuclear explosion, should you find yourself in the open at the moment of detonation, turn away from the flash immediately and adopt the basic defence posture behind any available natural shelter. Lie face-down on the ground, cover all exposed parts of the body with your clothes and close your eyes. Two minutes later don the protective gown and mask. If you are inside a building, get as far away as possible from all doors and windows. Crouch down close to a wall or crawl beneath a piece of furniture and adopt the basic defensive posture.'

If you survive, it's your turn and you get two rolls of the dice.

If the US is a human melting pot, then Eastern Europe is a scrap yard. There — a little of everything, here — not enough of anything. I'm having a drink with a Croat and a Bosnian and my two Serb mates. We converse in English and swear in our respective mother tongues. We reminisce about a sunken country

where the stars were red, the girls were roses, the young men were fiery, and the mountain goatherds swifter than mountain goats. This evening, here in the capital of the disunited states, parallel police lines meet. Drinking buddies from the two happiest barracks in the Peace Camp are winding their way home between piles of blackened snow. A chained dog barks in the dark yard. Not a word of it is true, howls Marko on all fours in the snow.

'Every day is today.'*

ugly, ulcer, ups-a-daisy, umbrella, undercover, undermine, Underground, understate, ultima ratio, unabridged, uncharted, unbound, unbooked, unwritten, unread, unready, unbirthday

I find Laci Márton, who has been considerate enough to buy two bottles of 'Grandson'.** We fling ourselves into the crowd and step out a kolo dance-step with our coats unbuttoned. A young girl in the crowd has a placard which says 'Marry me.' The revolutionary march is

---

*   W–G, p. 93.
** 'Unoka' is a Serb brand of grappa sold in miniature bottles in every corner shop.

the Bosnian Gypsy rumba from *Underground*. Mileta says everything makes sense at these moments. Belgrade is a place of the here and now. Windows were made to celebrate the crowds, streets were built for demos. If that is so, then some good must have come out of Trianon. The trigger pulled by Gavrilo, the Cold Days, the partisans, Tito — everything has to have a meaning. 1956, the Eastern Bloc, a picture dictionary for children, the Móra

Publishing House. Not forgetting the last window–giraffe, where a country can be assembled from words and a city from faces, where it is worth standing up to water cannons, getting oneself beaten up, scattering fliers to the wind, being active underground, organizing protests, getting arrested, getting released. It all had to happen: the Sarajevo assassination, the sniping in Bosnia, the concentration camps, the mass graves, Dayton, Milošević. Even Mira Marković has some sort of meaning at this moment. That, then, is what we suffered for.

And now, boys and girls, let us hold hands and look one another in the eye. It's all the faces or none, for only together can we pass through the bulletproof glass.

ú

úttörő = Pioneer
újságíró = journalist
útvesztő = maze

That era when, innocent and blind, we paved the way for a better future under the rubric of internationalism glows like my last Havana as I wait for the Yugoslav girl-comrades in front of the disco at the Pioneers' summer camp in the Buda hills. One by one, the girl-comrades slow-waltz with us, their tongues loosened by the foreign surroundings. At night we climb into Barrack Block Eight through an open window and scarper through a closed window when Ivan thinks they are on to us. The vacation comes to an end, so we send letters abroad, hoping that one day our sister troop will invite us to their place in return, when the girl-comrades will have rounded out more, and they'll play ABBA and Boney M. Back then a traveller knew what to expect, because on the pink-coloured half of the map the peace camp stood united. You all joined the same Party, lived in the same houses, were not afraid of the same big bad wolf, were treated the same in shops, and served the same soup with the same aluminium ladle. And somehow, despite apparent differences, hamburgers, *zmrzlna*, that unpronounceable Czech ice cream, the currywurst on Alexanderplatz, Romanian whisky and canned Albanian clams all had something in common. They all contained that same indefinable je ne sais quois, which did not intrinsically belong to them, something indisputably other-worldly which, no matter how much one chewed it, always congealed into a single block in our mouths.

'KLÁRI: Give it to me!
JÁNOS: What?
KLÁRI: That thingy . . .'*

---

* 'The word "thingy" should be avoided if at all possible.' W–G, p. 71.

A Pioneer, that's me! Brave and intrepid. What's there to be scared of? My fifty-five pounds are utopia made flesh. I ceaselessly deepen my knowledge, willingly and cheerily, along with friendship between nations. A Pioneer, that's me. Dib, dib, dib — dob, dob, dob. I lend a hand wherever I can — to you, and you, and you too! You didn't get into trouble for nothing. I'm steadfast as the trust endowed upon me, as upon all of you too. One tug on my neckerchief and the reactionaries scatter, sobbing all the way home.

The Pioneer movement was also popular in Yugoslavia. Nevertheless there were certain differences, such as the Space Pioneers who learned all about space, spacecraft and space dogs. The Moondogs, as they were called, vied with each other in annual trials of strength. Once a school from the mountains of

Montenegro won and was awarded a brand-new Cesna, in working order. Since they didn't have an airport, they pushed their prize up the mountain — an entire troop of ten-year-old Pioneers, little Sisyphuses rolling a Cesna up a Montenegrin hillside. The plane has stood there ever since, though it gets a wash from time to time. The children have grown up now, but the Cesna has never

flown. After all, it wasn't quite the steed they'd bargained for.

UFO, utopia, universe, uniform, urine, usual, user, USSR

The Pioneers' Twelve Rules, unlike the prescriptive Ten Commandments, reflected a descriptive world view. They dangled an already consummated future before our eyes. A Pioneer is a fully fledged, perfect being and acts like one by, for instance, always telling the truth — Rule Six. I'd rather have the New Testament any day. If a stone is thrown at you, throw bread in return. Just great! When a Creator runs out of ideas bun-fights are always an option, then it descends into farce. But what if a Pioneer says all Pioneers are liars? Because everyone knows Sohár tells fibs, even if he does have a red tie and a whistle. It's a nice whistle but Sohár doesn't deserve it. One has to admit the Pioneer is only human. That could be Rule Thirteen. Then again, it's so obvious it doesn't need a separate point. Rule Thirteen remains unspoken. We all have our weak points. I, for one, stole a logic game and hid it in my sock. I was only a Little Drummer at the time, and my parents made me return it, but you could tell they were really proud because in those bright red circles and triangles they saw their son's unquenchable thirst for knowledge. As for stealing, there was no rule about that, it was built into the system.

Ü

We were on holidays in the Seventies. At a summer resort on Luppa Island, just north of Budapest. The window looked out on the Danube, but I didn't, because I was too short and couldn't reach it. Nor did my parents, they played cards in the lounge instead. There was also a barbecue and a ping-pong table in this works holiday camp, where we had a holiday voucher paid for by the trade union because we had earned it. We went there to rest. I couldn't imagine what on earth I needed a rest from, but a voucher is a voucher, besides which I really should stop picking my nose or it'll end up like an elephant's trunk. What's more it was the end of the season. A wonder the Danube wasn't frozen over. I tried to spend my time in a dignified manner. I watched the matinees on TV: 'Captain Courageous' and the Soviet cartoon 'Hang on a Moment'. The rabbit wouldn't hang on even for a tick. I rooted for the wolf, but he kept on getting himself smashed up. That was something I could relate to even back then. I was already such a well-known figure in the A&E department at the János Hospital that my parents used to draw lots to decide who'd take me next time. The wolf smoked those cardboard-tipped tubes of *makhorka* whereas I had to eat carrots so I could whistle properly. I never did learn to whistle, however, and the wolf never did catch the rabbit. To my mind, the two things were somehow connected. Then came 'Small Films from the Big Wide World'. My show. Brandishing a half-ton sledgehammer above my head, I would swing it to the East, swing it to the West and say the magic words: *'vsyo khochu znat'.* I want to know everything! What happens to a frog if it's dipped in sulphur at minus two hundred degrees? What became of Laika the space dog? How many minutes are there in spring? Why do balding old men smile down from such huge bloody posters?

Which team will I root for in the Soviet-US ice hockey match? What do Mum and Dad do when they're not doing anything?

There was a repeat of the TV exercise show 'You're Not Too Old to Start'. My parents didn't start at all, whereas I was supposed to exercise to grow big. Like the carrots. And there in the lounge was the presenter of the show, Kati Makrai herself, along with her daughters, sitting and watching themselves on TV. When it got to the trunk circling movements they couldn't restrain themselves any longer and stood up to join in. On the TV they explained how to do it, and that's exactly what they did. You could tell it wasn't their first time. Grown-ups began to drift into the room, beer bottles in hand, fascinated by the interaction of film and real life. To me it was self-evident, like the teddy bear brushing his teeth before the evening children's story on TV: '*Gurgle, gurgle, phooey.*' The exercise girls were exercising. An idyllic socialist-realist tableau was framed in the doorway: the worker-peasant-intellectual staring slack-jawed at the first *live* broadcast of Hungarian television. The old codgers debated the merits of the evolutionary curve, from girlhood to

womanhood, while running on the spot, slurping beer through chapped lips. When they were out of breath my favourite came up: the deep-breathing exercise. Let's take a deep breath. Now, suck the air deep inside, one-two. Now, let it out slowly, three-four.

That very day I fell into the swollen Danube. My parents run along the bank shouting. The water seeps slowly through the multiple layers of pullovers. I begin to sink: '*Gurgle, gurgle, phooey*', I take a deep breath. I am of the world and the world is mine. The water carries me away, cap on my head, pom-pom on the cap. What can possibly go wrong? Before I go under I feel a thrilling lukewarm sensation in my groin. They pull me out and hug me, plunge me into hot water then yank me out of that too. They rub me from head to toe, kiss me again and hug me again. They want to give me a treat. Anything I want, I can have.

'"I brought you something", Péter's father says. Péter does not know yet what it is. Maybe a bag of sweets, maybe a live rabbit, or perhaps a pencil.'*

Borka is organizing a debate in the Pavilion on whether theatres have the right to strike. Ljubiša Rištić, the legendary actor and avant-garde director turned member of the Politburo, arrives late. He abuses Danilo Kiš's widow for a while then turns to Filip. I like you, Ljubiša tells him, but you understand nothing. You don't see what's going on around

* W–G, p. 151.

here. A politically compromised actress makes a scene. The theatre is the very air she breathes. Surely they're not asking her to stop breathing? A pamphlet was published about the evening. In my contribution 'urban' was mistakenly translated as '*über*', which elegantly rendered my entire account meaningless. The government paper calls me naive and sentimental, the biggest opposition paper applauds me. At the press conference a journalist asks whether there might be some misunderstanding about my name. The Zilahy is fine, but shouldn't that be Lajos?

ű

űr = space
űr = blank
űr = nothingness

I went out for cigarettes, but the pedestrian street had been blocked off. Parallel police cordons stand back to back, a few feet of no-man's land between them. In the no-man's land there's a cigarette kiosk, just out of reach, as though magnified through a plexiglas shield darkly. Several things then happen simultaneously. I get a craving for nicotine, and I long for the kiosk lady, who is stranded in a commercial vacuum. Only her head and chest are visible, like a magazine cover. She doesn't move and foreign bodies accumulate around her. Before our very eyes the Belgrade riot-cops are giving birth to their most stylish installation to

date. They carve an arbitrary slice out of the city, not to use it but to create a show-piece. The area under surveillance becomes an exhibit from which all protesters have been cleared. The empty pedestrian street is a statement, providing an emphatic counterpoint to the single spot into which the protesters are crowded. The riot cops are not part of but a border to this virtual world. They mark out an ideal space, henceforth liberated from the status of being a public area, its molecules now vibrating on a different plane. At the centre of this Cordon Art stands the unattainable object, and within it the kiosk lady, floating in a con-

sumer vacuum, unable to sell so much as a box of matches. And into this vacuum that is waiting to be filled a lone protester pours his desire. He gazes with yearning at the Rousseauesque little garden in the urban miasma, with its treasure-trove of cigarettes, cigars, colour film, slivovitz, glossy magazines, chocolates, chewing gum and sweets. As consumer power grows within the crowd of protesters, the symbolic space under police protection transforms into an anti-capitalist performance — a lonely cigarette kiosk orbiting in space. Then a balloon wobbles into the air space and lands in the public vacuum on the far side of the cordon. The balloon adds a new dimension to the emptiness of the empty space with the problem of how hermetically it can be sealed off. The empty space is filled with an empty space. There is nothing inside the balloon, yet it's full.

The balloon carries information too, an inscription in black felt-tip pen: 'Long live the fallen heroes! Close down the airport! Keep going, colleagues, I've almost found myself a chick!'

V

vár = castle
vér = blood
vámpír = vampire
vörös csillag = red star
valahol = somewhere

When we got to the Turkish wars, it occurred to me that castles were only mentioned when they were being destroyed, the defenders were generally put to the sword. Castle and defenders appeared at the moment of their disappearance. A castle is the architecture of demolition, it is built to be destroyed. This phenomenon can be observed in its purest form on the beach. Sandcastles, castles in Spain, castles in the air.

Belgrade Castle was built on a hill at the junction of two rivers. In the castle there is a tank museum. In the early Nineties, tanks could be seen on the streets too. That's also when water cannons were first used. The closest functioning water cannon to Budapest is to be found in Belgrade. When the temperature drops below zero water freezes and crystallizes. When that happens you can see ice on a lot of beards.

The cabby does not smoke, because it might damage his health, but he asks for the pack anyway to see what I wanted to pass off on him. I'm getting uptight, but then he nods, OK, which means I'm OK too, not junk. You have to check everything to see if it's for real, the cabby says. Ever since the embargo he's been suffering from a distinct lack of reality. Money has no value, only blood has collateral to back it up. Real blood has to be shed.

The news bulletin begins at seven-thirty. Armed with whistles, pots and wooden spoons, we march out onto Filip's balcony. Bilbo is the official dog mascot for the demos and has a certificate to prove it. We beat the enamel pots, the dog stands on its hind legs, barking, and then we launch into a wild voodoo dance of exorcism. The terrace door across the street opens, a man comes out with a wooden spoon and a pot. That's Đilas's son, Filip says. VOOODOO!!! We're doing voodoo for a free press, to exorcize the evil from television, the devils from hell, the poison from potassium cyanide, the shrill ringing from the trams, the growl from the tiger in your tank, the rain from the clouds, mother's milk from nursing breasts, peril from the seas.

Dejan Bulatović, a schoolboy, was tortured by the cops during his interrogation because in a demo he walked around with a Milošević puppet dressed in prisoner's clothes. The heavies who interrogated Bulatović insist they did nothing to B. that B. did not do to the puppet.

via, villa, vine, view, village, vigour, vertigo, virgin, victor, victim, visor, Venus, vengeance, vortex, voodoo, voyage, vaudeville, vampire

Belgrade's victory memorial was supposed to stand on Terazije, in the city centre, but the rival parties could not agree upon whose headquarters the statue should face. A poet suggested that the statue should be placed on a revolving pedestal, but then it supposedly became a problem that the sculptor had made its genitals too big. In the end the statue was set on top of a tall column on the castle's ramparts, above the confluence of the Danube and the Sava. There stands Victor, grasping the hilt of his sword in his hand.

In bygone days people lauded Belgrade for its location. The Turks reckoned that the vista from its hilltop prompted one to contemplation. This is where sultans hatched plans to conquer Europe. It is also where Hunyadi chewed over the possibility of reconquering the Balkans and where, of a morning, the student leader Čedomir Jovanović can be seen sitting on a wall. This is where I'm dangling my feet, at the confluence of the two rivers, at the foot of Victor and his giant prick, wondering what can be done with forty-four letters in the city of Belgrade.

The tale of Milošević and Marković is a romantic love story. A Communist Bonnie and Clyde, they met in a seminar at the Party Academy. One was called Freedom, the other Peace. They faced the future together. Slobo walked Mira home and promised never to leave her, not even if she should join another party, whereas Mira promised to stay with him even if there were no stars left in the sky. Mira's father had been a partisan, fighting with Tito. Her mother was killed by the Germans. She was an informer, but after she'd informed on all her friends, she became redundant. Mira announced that they would never relinquish the power they had won through blood sacrifice, except through blood sacrifice. In answer, the university students organized a blood donation drive to facilitate a decision. They managed to collect nearly one hundred pints, but the Party would have none of the voluntary blood sacrifice. The students are giving blood to those in power. But what do they want in return?

'The colour crimson looks like this: It is darker than scarlet red. The five-pointed red star and the red flag are emblems of the working class.'*

With garlic and holy water, they try to exorcize the dean from the university. They light candles and cross themselves. The holy water is straight from St. Mark's. Vampire is the only Serbian word that has spread across the world. Vampires are immortal or, to be more accurate, they can die only if they are killed, which is complicated by the fact that they are dead to begin with. In order to be rid of a vampire, he must be pierced through the heart with a stake carved from thorn-apple wood. Vampires are not wild animals, they depend on man for their sustenance. They live and die around the house, imbibing blood and sleeping in their coffins. Vampires are sound sleepers. The common history of vampire and man goes back to the beginning of time. It is impossible to decide who domesticated whom. The vampire inspires fear and strengthens community ties. The vampire is a factor in civilisation, an Eastern European monster who became a success story in the West. During the election campaign, Šešelj's men marched to Tito's grave with a six-foot-long stake in order to exhume the

*   W–G, p. 156.

beach in California. Enthusiastic conservationists drag it back to the sea. On Channel Two a documentary. Somewhere in the world, a man is killed every second. Or just a film on television.

W

WC = WC
whisky = whisky
Winston = Winston
Woodstock = Woodstock

ex-Yugoslav vampire, run him through the heart, cut off his head and incinerate his body, so people might sleep in peace. The show featured the swastika, the hammer and sickle, a papal tiara and the skull-and-crossbones. According to an obscure tradition, a white horse is first transformed into a black moth, and vampires come from black moths, as every child knows. It is possible that this rumour was spread around by the followers of Svatopluk on account of a dodgy real-estate deal that he made.* The story provides no guidance on what to do should you come across a pupated white horse.

This book is all about choices. You have to make choices even when there is nothing to choose from. The favourite song of the protesters is based on a pun: 'I can't sing because they've stolen my voice.' MTV made a clip from it. In Serbian, 'voice' and 'vote' are the same word.

Somewhere in the world people are protesting, someone is being beaten up, the news bulletin drones on through dinner. The baby is screaming, so it's impossible to hear who, where or why. Amateur footage shows a man's head being repeatedly kicked. Burma? Biafra? Belgrade? A surging crowd throws itself at shields. Then the placid features of the news reader. A dolphin has become stranded on a

Winston, the taste of freedom, said fifty years ago that from Stettin to Trieste an iron curtain was descending across the Continent. His name doubly fitted him for victory. Winston parts his stubby fingers, the other 'V' is holding a cigar. He was born with that double 'V', while we, the victims (single v), watched from a country that fell apart into one piece to see what would happen next. During the war Winston had a WC in his bunker. He had a direct line to Roosevelt in a small room, a well-kept secret, so he could listen to the promptings from the other shore.

Winston with Golden Gate, surrounded by ten thousand helmets. He has a rubber truncheon thrown at him and is asked to give it back, then chased into a pub, dragged out by the hair and beaten until he starts begging for

---

* Svatopluk was a ninth-century Slav chief who ceded to the Magyars lands they were seeking to conquer. Legend has it that they merely asked him for some water and soil in exchange for a white horse.

113

mercy, whereupon the efforts are redoubled. If Winston is the taste of freedom, then what the hell were we smoking before? All day we never gave it a second thought: we brushed our teeth, wiped our asses, lit up and puffed. Always with the same gesture. Now it's a commercial break. I've seen the ad a thousand times, but only now do I notice the caption at the bottom: CAN SERIOUSLY DAMAGE YOUR HEALTH!

Back home in Hungary, for any demo with more than one hundred people toilets have to be laid on so that the alternative thinkers don't piss all over town. Here in Belgrade, trusting to the good will of the caterers who have rallied to their support, the opposition have not put up portaloos. The wooden toilets of the riot cops stand in front of the presidential palace: blue, transportable riot-cop karzeys, in case of an emergency. The first dog turd appears at the foot of the gentle, snow-covered slopes of Pioneers Park, worming its way towards the light with a writhing motion, its exhalations defrosting a palm-sized area of green around itself, a springtime sense of *déjà vu*, a piece of Budapest after the thaw.

During the long hot summer of '89 the Serbian mass transportation system achieved its most impressive victory over time, which had seemingly stood still. On the sesquicentennial of the collapse of Serbia a song entitled 'Slobodan, They Call You Freedom' blasts from loudspeakers on the field of the battle of Kosovo. Milošević arrives in a helicopter, wipes the sweat from his brow, delivers a short speech, then flies up, up and away. There are more people than at Woodstock. The participants are given packed lunches, there's an ox bake, camp fires, folk dance troupes — a cultural display to satisfy any heart. Milošević claims that the problems aren't half as bad as they seem, we can solve them if we want to — provided we are willing to make sacrifices. Now the time has come for sacrifices, just like six hundred years ago. We are facing new challenges, new struggles ahead. No-one will ever beat you again, Milošević promises.

The future is beautiful, and it's just around the corner. Make war, not love — Serbia's Woodstock, 28 June 1989. During the festivities, not one single baby was born.

wacko, wanton, wanted, walrus, Wall Street, wallet, walky-talkie, Waltzing Matilda, Wandering Jew, Wellington, water cannon, war criminal, words, words, words

A bottle of whisky is passed around: a gangster has come down to join the demonstration. Heavy gold chain, big cross. He offers me a cigar and asks what I, as a foreign correspondent, think of Belgrade women. He asks every foreigner at the demo. That's his thing, the women of Belgrade. We have a swig of whisky and, with a bunch of schoolgirls giggling behind us, send smoke rings floating over the cordon.

X

The umpteenth speaker in line is a noted author: earlier he was a follower of Milošević, then of Šešelj and currently of Drašković. He tells the crowd to be vigilant. He has a reputation for being very slick and nailing his enemies without qualms. Slick he may be, but is Mr. X slicker than Socrates?

y

The horseshoe-shaped item of equipment attached to the waist and used for passing the

ball into the hole in some pre-Columbian ball game was called a 'yugo'. The ball symbolized the Sun and so was not allowed to touch the ground. The captain of the losing team was beheaded. According to others, the winner was sacrificed, but how were the losers rewarded?

Z

zavar = jam
Zimony = Zemun
zűr = trouble

The radio is being jammed. It crackles as it announces that the Belgrade students have gone to the city's zoo in search of the dean. The ice on the Danube is breaking up, a boat is frozen in the river. This side is the other side. Across the way is the tower of Zemun, last bastion of the Monarchy. Electricity in the air, the sound of wild animals and melting ice.

ZS

zsarol = extort
zsargon = jargon
zsidó = Jew
zsiráf = giraffe

Excerpt from Croat television on Serb television: Tudjman declares in Serbo-Croatian that an international conspiracy and the Soros Foundation are behind the demonstrations in Belgrade.

P. S. Years later, as Colonel Aureliano Buendía stood in front of the firing squad, he recalled the summer afternoon when his father showed him what ice was.

Best wishes from your friend,

Péter

115

Biographical Index

Andrić, Ivo (1892–1975): Serbian fiction writer, winner of the Nobel Prize for Literature (1961). His best-known work is *The Bridge on the Drina*. A native of Bosnia whom the Croats have also avowed as being one of their own (in other words, he was Yugoslav).

Babić, Sava (b. 1934): Critic, translator, he instituted the Hungarian Department at the University of Novi Sad.

Babits, Mihály (1883–1941): One of Hungary's most distinguished pre-war poet-novelists.

Basara, Svetislav (b. 1953): *Enfant terrible* of Serbian literature; only one of his books has so far been published in English translation: *Chinese Letter*.

Csoma de Kőrös, Alexander (Sándor) (1784–1842): Transylvanian Hungarian oriental scholar who travelled by foot to the Indian-Tibetan border in search of the origins of the Magyars. Commissioned by the Asiatic Society of Bengal to compile the first English-Tibetan dictionary and book of grammar.

Đilas, Milovan (1911–95): Yugoslav Communist leader before turning author and dissident.

Đinđić, Zoran (1952–2003): A philosopher by profession, he was the politician who led the Democratic Opposition of Serbia coalition to power in the election of December 2000. As prime minister of Serbia he was responsible for handing over Milošević to face war crimes charges in The Hague and soon afterwards was assassinated.

Drašković, Vuk (b. 1946): A journalist then press adviser, his novels (*The Judge*, *Knife*, *Prayer* and *Russian Consul*) achieved some notoriety during the 1970s and '80s. With Vojislav Šešelj he co-founded the Serbian National Renewal Party in 1989. A central figure in the street protests described here, Drašković was the first political figure in Serbia to openly point to crimes by Serb forces. Presently Serbia's temporary minister of foreign affairs.

Gábor, Áron (1810–49): Transylvanian-born military engineer whose guns played a vital role in the victories won by General Bem's army for Hungary in its 1848–49 War of Independence against the Austrians.

Hegedušić, Krsto (1901–71): Naïve painter, Tito's favourite artist, of Hungarian origin (the name means 'fiddler').

Horn, Gyula (b. 1932): Hungary's minister of foreign affairs when the country decided to open its Austrian border to East Germans wishing to emigrate to West Germany in early autumn 1989. A founder of the Hungarian Socialist Party, he led a socialist-liberal coalition as prime minister (1994–98).

Hunyadi, John (János) (c. 1407–56): Voivode of Transylvania (1441–56), governor of Hungary (1446–52) then Captain-general of Hungary (1452–56).

Irinyi, János (1819–95): Hungarian chemist credited with inventing or perfecting a safety match in 1845.

Jakšić, Djuro (1832–78): Serb Romantic poet, prose writer and playwright.

Karadžić, Radovan (b. 1945): Psychiatrist, poet and politician, he was the first president of the Bosnian Serb administration in Pale after the break-up of Yugoslavia in 1992. Now on the run from arrest to face indictment for war crimes and genocide by the International Criminal Tribunal for the former Yugoslavia in The Hague.

Karadžić, Vuk (1787–1864): Serbian writer and folk song collector; Serbia's Brothers Grimm.

Kiš, Danilo (1935–89): Serbian fiction writer of Hungarian origin, best known for the novel *Garden, Ashes* and short-story collections *A Tomb for Boris Davidovich* and *The Encyclopedia of the Dead*.

Lezsák, Sándor (b. 1949): An author turned conservative politician who played a role in the negotiations with the Communist Party that paved the way for Hungary's change of régime in 1889–1990.

Liszt, Franz (Ferenc) (1811–86): Famous Hungarian composer also claimed by the Germans.

Marković, Mirjana (b. 1942): Now the widow of Slobodan Milošević, she is leader of the Yugoslav Communist Party in Serbia.

Márton, László (b. 1959): Hungarian writer and translator, whose novels include *The True Story of Jakob Wunschwitz* and the trilogy *Brotherhood*.

Mehmed or Mohammed II (1430–81): Turkish sultan (1451–81), who captured Constantinople (1453) and conquered the Balkans.

Milošević, Slobodan (1941–2006): President of Serbia (1989–97) and Yugoslavia (1997–2000), he was the leader of Serbia's Socialist Party from its foundation in 1992.

Miloš I Obrenović, Prince (1780–1860): Having fought Serbia's First Uprisings against the Turks to the end in 1813, he became Serbia's absolute ruler in 1815, ruling as prince until 1839 then again from 1858 to 1860.

Molnár, Ferenc (1878–1952): Hungarian writer, he is best known as a playwright for *Liliom* (1909), which provided the basic plot for Rogers and Hammerstein's 1945 musical *Carousel*, and as a novelist for *The Paul Street Boys* (1927).

Nazor, Vladimir (1876–1949): Croatian poet and novelist, he joined Tito's partisans at the age of sixty-six and after the war became president of the Praesidium of the Croatian Sabor.

Njegoš, Petar Petrović (1813–51): Poet and Montenegrin ruler; responsible for the first genocide of Muslims in modern European history.

Pavić, Milorad (b. 1929): Serbian fiction writer, author of the lexicon novel *Dictionary of the Khazars* and the tarot novel *Last Love in Constantinople*.

Peçevi, Ibrahim (1572–1650): A chronicler, famous for his two-volume history of the Ottoman Empire, he was born in the Hungarian town of Pécs (hence his name).

Pešić, Vesna (b. 1940): Civil rights activist, founding member of the Yugoslavian Helsinki Committee (1985) and of the Center for Anti-War Action in Belgrade (1991).

Peter I Karadjordjević (1844–1921): Grandson of the leader of the first revolt against the Turks, he reigned as King of Serbia (1903–21).

Petőfi, Sándor (1823–49): Hungarian Romantic poet (his father was Serbian with the family name Petrović), he became famous as the radical voice of Hungary's 1848 revolution.

Porogi, András (b. 1960): Hungarian high school teacher, later director of the Toldy Ferenc Gymnasium in Buda. Author of *Venus and Mars*, an award-winning collection of short stories.

Prodanović, Mileta (b. 1959): Serbian artist.

Rákóczi, Prince Francis II (1676–1735): Prince of Transylvania (1704–11), he led a War of Independence against the Habsburgs.

Rištić, Ljubiša (b. 1947): Serbian actor, writer, director; a vice-president in the Yugoslav Communist Party under Mirjana Marković.

Samardžić, Ljubiša (b. 1936): Serbian actor and director. Šurda was a role he took in a popular TV serial.

Sava, St (1175 or 76–1235): Considered the founder of the independent Serbian Orthodox Church. Originally Prince Rastko Nemanjić, son of Stefan Nemanja, Serbian, founder of the Serbian medieval state, and brother of Stefan Prvovenčanić, first Serbian king.

Šešelj, Vojislav (b. 1954): Politician, president of the Serbian Radical Party during the 1990s. He is now detained in The Hague under indictment for war crimes by the International Criminal Tribunal for the Former Yugoslavia

Sokollu, Mehmed-pasha (1506–79): Born in a Bosnian village (family name Sokolović), as a boy he was collected under the Ottoman 'blood tax' system and eventually rose to high office as grand vizier to three sultans.

Stephen Dušan, Tsar: Emperor of Serbia (reigned 1322–55).

Stephen I, King (Saint) (c. 974–1038): Founder of Hungary as a Christian state.

Strossmayer, Josip Juraj (1815–1905): Croatian Catholic priest, bishop of Djakovo in Slavonia, with jurisdiction over Bosnia and Hercegovina, from 1849, and also apostolic vicar for Serbia (1851–96).

Suleiman I, 'the Magnificent' (c. 1495–1566): Sultan of the Ottoman Empire (1520–66).

Šurda: Character played by Serbian actor Ljubiša Samardžić (b. 1936) in a popular TV serial entitled 'Hot Wind'.

Tandori, Dezső (b. 1938): *Enfant terrible* of Hungarian literature, aka Nat Droid, a prolific poet, fiction writer and translator and a nature lover.

Teller, Edward (Ede) (1908–2003): Hungarian-born 'father' of the hydrogen bomb.

Tito, Josip Broz (1892–1980): Member of Yugoslav Communist Party since early 1920s, he became its general secretary in 1937 and led partisan forces against Germany during the Second World War. He secured the country's independence from the USSR in 1948 and was first president of Yugoslav Republic (1953–80).

Vámbéry, Arminius (Ármin) (1831–1913): Famous Hungarian orientalist who was nicknamed 'The Dervish of Windsor Castle' on account of his close ties with the British Royal family.

Zilahy, Lajos (1891–1974): A middle-of-the-road Hungarian-born fiction writer, English translations of several of whose novels won a considerable readership in the UK both before and after the Second World War: *Two Prisoners* (1931), *The Deserter* (1932), *The Dukays* (1949) and *Century in Scarlet* (1966).

Zmaj, Jovan Jonavanović (1833–1904): Serb Romantic poet and translator (as well as a tractor model).

Zrinyi, Miklós (c. 1508–66): Hungarian statesman and military commander, he died breaking through the Ottoman troops of Suleiman I besieging the fortress of Szigetvár. His identically named great grandson (1643–1703) was Ban of Croatia and a noted poet who commemorated his deeds in *The Perils of Szigetvár*.

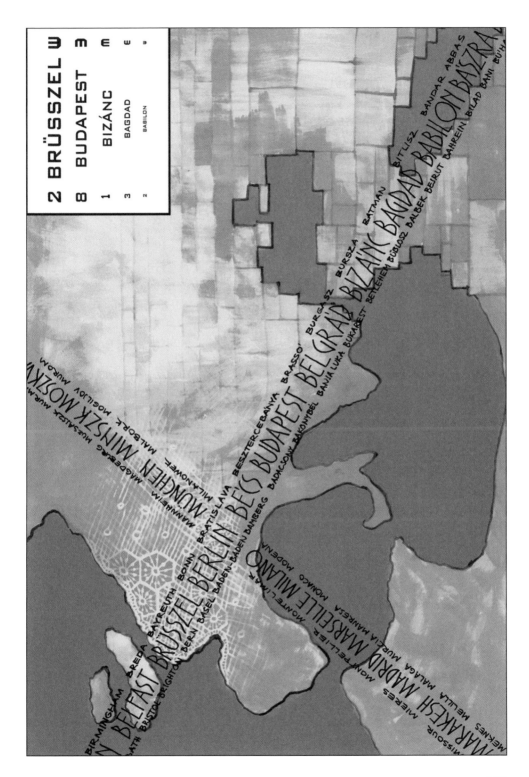

Peter Zilahy's award-winning books have been adapted into theater shows, radio plays, and a wealth of other media, inspired songs, and even flash mobs during the Orange Revolution in Ukraine, where *The Last Window-Giraffe* was Book of the Year. Zilahy is a versatile artist, whose work has been shown at The Kitchen in New York City, Ludwig Museum, Berliner Ensemble, Volksbühne, and The New Tretyakov Gallery, among others. He has performed on Broadway, lectured all over the world, was a Kluge Fellow at The Library of Congress, and a fellow of Akademie Solitude, handpicked by Nobel laureate Herta Müller. Zilahy joined Anthony Bourdain in Budapest for an episode of CNN's *Parts Unknown*.

About Sandorf Passage

Sandorf Passage publishes work that creates a prismatic perspective on what it means to live in a globalized world. It is a home to writing inspired by both conflict zones and the dangers of complacency. All Sandorf Passage titles share in common how the biggest and most important ideas are best explored in the most personal and intimate of spaces.